WARNING:

Teaching May Be Hazardous to Your Health

by William David

William David
Prince

Special thanks to:

Richard Freeman
Maria Agullo
Janet Montgomery
Melanie Heath-Jolly

ONE

I sat proudly at my desk admiring my stapler and tape dispenser. There was nothing special about either of them. They were not even new. It was what they symbolized. A blank grade book and a lesson plan book also sat on the old wooden desk, my desk. The building and other furnishings were old too, but I did not care. I had just been hired for my first real job and was now a fifth grade teacher at Kenwood Elementary School sitting in my quiet classroom for the first time. I was filled with a sense of achievement, and for the first time in my life felt like an adult. I had finally arrived. No one is really an adult simply by reaching a certain age. True adulthood also means being able to pay your own way through life. I now had a profession, a career, an income.

What to be when you grow up is a perplexing question for anyone. I suppose my career choice could partly be my grandmother's fault. I learned to speak at a very early age, and was told I did so at every opportunity. My grandmother, Mamau as I called her, suggested that I should get a job where I could talk for a living. I must have liked that idea because in junior high school I wanted to be a TV game show host. In high school, I went through a wanting to be an architect phase. I already wore thick glasses and my optometrist said all that close-up detail work could damage my eyes. I suppose most of the blame falls on my mother, a fourth grade teacher. One of the college classes I was taking required fifteen hours of community service. I volunteered at my mother's school and she asked me to tutor one of her students who had trouble reading. Having no pedagogical skills, I had nothing to go on but my own intuition. I did the best I could and after a while the boy showed noticeable improvement. I had no idea whether he just needed individual attention - many students do- or if he was just an extremely good actor. It gave me a sense of accomplishment and made me decide to do that for a living. My mother should have warned me.

Besides the worn teacher's desk, there were thirty-six student desks, two large dark green chalkboards with years of chalk dust still in the chalk trays, two large bulletin boards, and stacks of used textbooks on the floor lining the walls.

I recalled showing up at the school for my initial job interview. I saw a sweaty janitor in a dark gray jumpsuit pulling weeds in front of the school and asked him where the main office was. After politely thanking him I went inside. My education professors said to become friendly with the secretary and janitors because they were the most important people in the school. Boy was that right. He wasn't a janitor at all, he was the principal.

Teachers in Florida have a pre-planning week of preparation before the students begin. Too much of that time was wasted by long pointless meetings when we needed to decorate our rooms and plan our curriculums. In elementary school, classroom teachers taught reading, math, language arts, science, and social studies, so required lesson plans in each subject took time to prepare.

My fellow teachers were a lot more experienced and several offered to help but were too busy getting their own classrooms in order to actually assist me. More to the point, I was too embarrassed to ask for help because I did not want them to know how little I knew. I didn't even know how much I didn't know.

I never liked decorating bulletin boards so always looked for simple ideas. Besides hanging the alphabet on the walls above the bulletin boards, in both cursive and manuscript, I decorated one board with pictures of race cars and motorcycles for the boys and pictures of teen idols for the girls on the other.

I had just stapled a picture of a long-haired blond boy with a wide toothy smile and a low-cut shirt that I had found in a teenybopper magazine onto the bulletin board when Mrs. Sirota walked in.

"A few of us are going out to lunch. Would you like to join us?" asked the sixth grade teacher. "I suggest you do because once school starts you won't be able to do that for a while."

I had to check my wallet before I could answer. "Well, it looks like you caught me on a good day. I'd love to join you."

"Good. Let's go in my car."

As soon as her car pulled out of the school parking lot, she began sharing useful advice that I needed and never heard in any of my education classes in college.

"First, after you've explained the directions at least three times, don't be surprised when someone raises their hand and asks what they are supposed to do."

When we walked into the restaurant and joined a few other teachers, she said, "I was just warning him to never let the students see him smile the first two weeks of school."

"She's right," agreed Mr. Montgomery, "it excites the Munchkins. They'll think you're a soft pushover and walk all over you. And, just like you give a weekly spelling list and a spelling test, give them 6 to 8 weekly vocabulary words and test them on the definitions. I learned that the hard way. I spent a full period talking about how the pyramids were built, how tall they were, where the stones to build them came from, how they were transported, and how many workers it took to build them.

At the end, one student raised his hand and asked, 'What's a pyramid?' I had wasted the whole class. Never assume they already know the basics. Oh, and bring your own lunch from home. School cafeteria food is only a real treat if you love the flavor of sawdust."

"I saw your class list hanging on your door. Watch out for Earl Copeland and Blaine Osteen," warned Mrs. Hendricks. "They were both in my class last year. Those two addlepated boys would make a great advertisement for retroactive birth control. My fear of jail is the only reason they lived through the year."

"One more thing," added Mr. Montgomery. "If you ever want to try something new, it's easier to get forgiveness in this business than it is permission. Remember that."

Some of the younger teachers grumbled about the principal not thinking blue jeans looked professional. They wanted to wear them because sometimes they sat on the floor with the kids. It didn't bother me because I didn't have any blue jeans. My mother was raised in rural Kentucky where most men were either farmers or coal miners and wore blue jeans every day. Both were honorable occupations, but mother wanted me to have an easier life than that. She tossed out my blue jeans when I was around ten years old and I didn't even notice. That was partly because mine were hand-me-downs from my uncle who liked to pick on me. I think blue jeans are perfect for hard dirty work or hard dirty play, but I don't want any part of hard dirty work or hard dirty play.

That lunch was more enlightening than all my education classes put together.

I did not sleep well that night because I was worried about Meet Your Teacher Day. All week long I had been worried about how parents would feel about their son or daughter having an inexperienced teacher who was so young. I was only ten or twelve years older than my soon-to-be students.

Meet Your Teacher hours were from one o'clock until three. It could best be described as controlled chaos. It worked like an Open House with people coming and going as they pleased. I stood behind a table covered with student textbooks, sign-up sheets, and hand-outs. Sometimes five or six parents all wanted to talk to me at the same time, and other times I would be staring at the walls of my empty room. Most parents were much more interested in talking to each other than in meeting me. None seemed even remotely concerned about my age and most did not seem at all interested in what I would teach. They mainly wanted a copy of the school supply list and seemed thrilled that school was starting again. By three o'clock I had met the parents of about two/thirds of my students.

"It's always like this when it gets this way," said Mrs. Johnson.

Huh, meaningless doublespeak I thought.

"It looks like you had a good turn-out," she continued.

"I had three angry mothers, but it wasn't because of me. They were upset about the time and thought it should be in the evening so they wouldn't have to take time off from their jobs."

"I can understand that. I had a few of those too."

"Overall I thought it went well."

"Have a great weekend. Get lots of rest, and I'll see you on Monday."

Unfortunately I did not have much of a social life. After graduating from Florida Atlantic University, I moved back home with my parents to save for a down payment on a house.

Monday morning could not get here fast enough.

I stood at the door as each student walked into my classroom and was surprised that so few of them were wearing new clothes. My parents saw to it that I began every school year with new school clothes. Instead of excitement, the students seemed to have a resigned indifferent attitude.

After taking attendance and sending the lunch count to the cafeteria, I faced the class with a mixture of nervousness and excitement. Other than internship I had no experience as a teacher, but I had taken a theater class in college and been in a few plays. When the tardy bell rang, the symbolic stage lights came on, the curtain went up, and I *acted* like a teacher. I knew I was faking it and hoped my students could not tell.

"Welcome to the fifth grade, my name is Mr. Williams. School is about learning. If you leave the fifth grade without learning something, I have failed. I don't want to fail. I also know that sometimes people might be too shy to ask a question. That's what this is for," I said, holding up a metal box with a slit in the top. "Write any question you may have on a piece of paper and slip it into this box. No one is ever to open the box but me. Here's the best part, you don't have to put your name on it if you want it to be private. Even if you don't have a question but want to tell me something, just put it in here. You can even tell me a good joke. Please give it a try, even if you just want to say 'hello'."

After a brief introduction, I gave them three activity sheets to occupy their hands while I went over the classroom and school rules.

It suddenly dawned on me that I had thirty-six student desks and only thirty-five students on my class list, yet every desk was full. I quickly counted the desks to see if one of them had been removed. No, there were still thirty-six. I called the roll again asking each student to stand up when I called their name instead of answering 'here.' When I got to Janet Patrick, two girls stood up.

"Wait, you're both named Janet Patrick?"

Both girls nodded.

"Oh my. I only have one Janet Patrick on my roll, so there's been a mistake somewhere." Not knowing what else to do, I quickly decided to turn the problem over to someone else. "You're not in trouble, but I'm sending you to the office so they can figure this out."

One girl looked unphased by it but the other looked on the verge of tears. I walked over and tried to reassure her that everything would be OK. One Janet Patrick did not know where the office was; the other Janet Patrick did.

The girls returned about twenty minutes later along with Mrs. Heath-Jolly, the school secretary. She explained that one girl's family moved from Nebraska over the summer and when they saw her name on my class list, assumed that her old school had already enrolled her in our school. The office decided to move the new Janet to Mrs. Johnson's classroom across the hall.

The rest of the day, and the next, went surprisingly smooth. I was beginning to think that being a teacher was way easier than I ever expected.

By Wednesday my students were feeling more comfortable. Their idyllic facades began to melt, and they became much more talkative.

I told them to stop talking, and hoped they did, but had

little idea what to do if they did not. I was not sure if I was doing a poor job of controlling my class or if my expectations were too high and this was normal behavior.

In college, my professors talked a lot about the importance of classroom management. They mainly focused on furniture arrangement, how the room was decorated, and planned activities. The most practical thing they said was if two kids talked too much, separate them to different places in the room. They also stressed that there were bad parents, bad principals and even bad teachers, but there was no such thing as a bad child. If a student does not behave, look at yourself first. It is a sign that your lessons are not interesting enough or not being taught at the right level. I ended my first student-contact day filled with elation; I ended the first week filled with self-doubt.

Kenwood Elementary School was in a lower, working-class neighborhood where little value was placed on education. Most kids thought school was a punishment for being young, something to be endured until they were old enough to get a job. Not surprisingly, students were much more interested in talking to their friends than in learning.

"I hope everyone had a good weekend," I said standing in front of my class on Monday morning. "I think we need to add two new items to our list of class rules. First, a few of you handed in papers last week without putting your name on it, and most of you only wrote your first name. Ricky or Betty might work in kindergarten, but you are growing up and part of that means using your last name too. Your **first and last name** should always be the first mark on **EVERY** paper you turn in with two exceptions. It's the last thing you write when writing a letter, we'll talk about that in a few minutes, and you don't need to sign it at all when you put a note in the question box.

Second, last week I heard a few of you say some very mean things to each other. When I said something about it, you said you were just teasing. Teasing can be a lot of fun, but it can also hurt people's feelings. Sometimes I like to tease people and even enjoy being teased, but only by people who I know like me. If I'm not sure the teaser likes me, then it can hurt my feelings. Yes, grown-ups get our feelings hurt too, we're just better at hiding it.

There are a lot of funny jokes out there. For example,

Clyde has a big nose, but the other kids at his bus stop don't mind a bit because when it rains they can all stand under it and keep dry. Clyde's nose is so big his teacher won't let him sit on the front row because when he shakes his head, he erases the chalkboard. Those are funny unless Clyde really does have a big nose, then it's **mean**. I want to be the meanie in this room, not you. So never tease anyone you don't like, and never tease someone about a real weakness."

It was time to move on to the letter writing lesson. I explained the five parts of a letter: return address, date, greeting, body, and closing. Then told them about my fifth grade teacher having us write to the President of the United States. We actually received a reply from the White House a few months later. They were not interested in writing to the President but did agree to write to the Queen of England.

The students had just started writing when the fire alarm went off. I knew a fire drill was coming but did not know the exact time.

"Line up, single file! No talking! Last one out, turn the lights off."

We walked outside and stood waiting for the 'all clear' bell. I later learned that I was supposed to bring my grade book and take attendance again just in case someone was in the restroom or clinic. It was another of many things all teachers were supposed to know, but no one ever tells you.

We returned and I walked around the room as they resumed writing their letters. Some of the students looked lost in a fantasy of living in a palace with servants to wait on them.

Dear Queen,

You wear a long dress a lot. How do you keep it clean? When I wear a long dress, I get the bottom dirty.

Judy Charles

Dear Your Majesty,

You have a very large house. How do you keep it warm? Our house is always cold in the winter.

Steve Edwards

Dear Queen,

It must be fun to boss people around and have servants and cut people's heads off. Please write to me and send a picture.

Eric McCoy

I put all the letters into a large envelope addressed simply to Buckingham Palace, London, England, and took it to the post office on the way home from school.

The next morning I was grading math papers when the students walked in and did not look up until the tardy bell rang. I was shocked to see Blaine Osteen sitting at his seat in the back of the room with his shirt wide open and his bare chest exposed. My eyes bugged out, I stiffened my back and tried to pull off my best outraged teacher impersonation.

"How dare you come into my class like that! Get up here, now!"

As the pale-blond haired boy slowly walked forward, I

realized that this was the first time I had ever seen him in anything but an old dirty T-shirt that he would wear for a week at a time. I could recognize the stains.

"Oh, what happened to your buttons?"

"Mom used them for my sister's dress."

"Well that's not your fault. I guess you'll have to make do."

I felt horrible and wished I had never drawn attention to it.   My parents were not wealthy, but I never had to do without. For the rest of the day whenever I looked in his direction, he had one hand holding the shabby shirt together.

The next day Blaine came to school in the same shirt again. His mother had poked holes where the buttons should be and tied his shirt closed with a shoelace.

The first chance I had I went to Mrs. Sirota's class and asked if she had a few minutes to talk. I told her about what happened with Blaine and that I was planning to buy him a shirt with my own money.

"I had Blaine's older sister in my class two years ago. They're a very poor family. All seven of them live in a tiny rundown home in a migrant camp. Several of the windows are broken and they just leave them that way. In winter they block the openings with cardboard. They don't even have their own bathroom and share a communal bathroom with the other cabins. Most of the homes in the camp, shacks really, are only filled during harvest season, but the Osteens live there year-round. Don't waste your money on a new shirt, his mom will only sell it."

"Wow, I had no idea!"

"It get's even worse. The mother has strange priorities. Last year I saw her drive up to school in a brand-new car that she paid cash for. Both parents are just laborers in an orange grove, so their income is very low. I can't imagine how they saved enough for that car."

"How can people live like that? I don't understand."

"I don't know either, but if that shirt thing happens again, just send him to the clinic. They have extra clothes there in case kids have accidents."

"I'm getting the impression there must be at least a hundred things like that I'm supposed to know, but no one has ever told me."

"There's way more than a hundred, but you'll learn them eventually just like the rest of us did."

"I was going to ask Mr. Ackley for some advice, but since I'm here anyway I'll ask you instead. My class just ignores me when I ask them to stop talking. I feel like I'm yelling at them and I don't like that. How can I get them to stop talking so much?"

"I know exactly what you're saying. You're asking them to stop talking and, hope they do, but feel helpless if they don't, so you get louder. All beginning teachers go through that. You can't ask them to get quiet, you have to tell them. It may take a while, but you'll hit a point where you can't take it any longer. Something inside you will change and you will demand, not ask. That's when things change, and it happens all of a sudden. At least that's how it happened for me. Don't go to the principal about it. It's not a good idea to go to the person who evaluates you to ask for help. Why give them anything they could use it against you?"

The other fifth grade teachers thought it was best to stay

in our homeroom groups for the first two weeks so we could get to know our students better. Then we would start ability grouping for reading and math. To avoid embarrassing the kids in lower groups, the groups were named after colors. Mr. Montgomery joked about calling them gold, silver, bronze, and tarnished copper. We ended up calling them the red, yellow, green, and blue groups. I was given the red (high) reading group and the blue (low) math group.

All the students in the high reading group read at grade level or above so I decided they needed enrichment. Thanks to the school librarian's help, who called in assistance from other schools, we managed to borrow enough books for each student in the red group to have a copy of **Bunnicula**, by James Howe. It is a funny book about a vegetarian vampire rabbit who sucks the juice out of vegetables turning them white. It is even funnier because the story is told from the point-of-view of the family's dog. I laughed out loud several times when reading it to the class during my internship.

I took the opposite approach to the blue math group. They obviously did not gain much from textbooks, so I took a hands-on approach. I gathered addition, subtraction, multiplication, and division flash cards, play money to practice making change, cardboard teaching clocks with moveable hands, and a cardboard thermometer with a movable red and white elastic band so the kids could practice telling time and temperature. There was a bit of noise but the students were on task. I was happy as long as the principal did not walk in because principals don't usually like noise.

I am pretty good with faces but have never been good at remembering names. Now with new students in my reading and math classes, it was hopeless. I was making up names for everyone, Hilda, Gertrude, Sylvia, Buford, Ferdinand, and Eustice. It became a running joke.

Time has taught me that it is every teacher's nightmare when a former student comes up and asks, 'Do you remember me? What's my name?' Even teachers with great memories for names cringe because few people still look the same as they did in elementary school, especially girls who now have different hair styles and wear makeup.

I was still saving for a down payment on a house so was

looking forward to the Parade of Homes this weekend where builders show off their best efforts in hopes of strumming up business. I was hoping to find ideas to help me decide which features I wanted and which ones I did not. One home was decorated with a dragon fly in every room, whether it was an embroidered pillow, a picture hanging on the wall, or a broche pinned to a curtain. Another home had a poolside bar. I fell in love with the bar stools. They were tall director's chairs and I knew I had to have one for my classroom. I could sit on it and still be tall enough to see everyone.

I took the canvas seat and back panels to a hardware store and so they could apply press-on letters for the words 'Keep Off' on the seat, and my name on the back panel. The other teachers referred to it as my throne. The kids loved pointing out that my chair read, 'Mr. Williams Keep Off.'

Another of many frustrations for a classroom teacher were pull-out programs. Students identified with special needs were pulled out at various times during the day by certified teachers and aides for tutoring in reading or math, speech therapy, physical or occupational therapy, and counseling in personal or emotional problems. Bright students with IQs over 130 were pulled out too for gifted classes. The students genuinely needed the extra help, but it is hard to teach students who are not in the room.

Mrs. Taylor showed up at my door to collect Mark and Blaine for reading remediation.

"What class are they missing?" she asked.

"This is science," I replied.

"How are their grades in science?"

"What do you mean how are their grades? They're not here during science."

"Let me guess, nobody told you. I used to be a new teacher too. You have to give them individual lessons in whatever class they're pulled out of. And don't forget, you have to record those lessons in your plan book. I'll help you get started."

Not only did I have to plan and record all my regular lessons, now I had to plan and record my mini-lessons for the pull-out students. Lesson plans were very important and ALWAYS needed to be prepared in advance. They also needed to be kept in a prominent place in the classroom so a substitute

could easily find them and know what to do. We had to turn

them into the office every Friday before we went home so the

principal to check them.

My students always loved it when I read notes from the

question box. I scanned them first so I would not embarrass

anyone or reveal anything personal. Several of the class clowns

started putting in more provocative notes just to see if I had the

courage to read them out loud.

I was surprised by the number of love letters I received.

Some were signed, most were not. In one note a girl asked me to

marry her mother, whom I had never met, because she wanted

me to be her father. I even took a few home to share with my

parents and grandparents.

Dear Mr. Williams,

I love you, lovely man. I love slick

hair like yours. When I turn eighteen, will

you marry me? Yes_____ or No_____

Do you love me? Yes_____ or No _____

Dear Mr. Williams,

I love you more than ever.

You are so handsome, man have I got a crush on you! I love you verrrry much, really I do. Cause I love you, hope to see you soon.

Bye Cuttie Pie

With Lotts of *Love*

Secret Admirer ?????

P.S.

I love you with all my heart.

I love Mr. Brenford Williams

Hope you're not married!

I want to marry you when I get eighteen.

Okay Honey Sugar Pie?

Maybe she was not the greatest letter writer, but I had to admire her taste in men.

"You better keep an eye on this one," said my grandmother after reading one of the love letters.

"I'm twenty-two years old and she's only eleven."

"She'll get over that," replied my grandmother.

Things seemed to go relatively smoothly for the next few weeks. After returning to school on a Monday, I heard a few students discussing their weekends as they walked into my room.

"My grandfather shot my father."

"My father shot my mother's boyfriend."

"My house burned down."

I thought it was some kind of weird macabre game of 'can you top this' until lunch.

"I hear some of your kids had a busy weekend," said Mr. Montgomery.

"What do you mean?" I lived in a nearby town so did not always hear the local gossip.

"You haven't heard?" said Mrs. Sirota. "Bruce Falwell's parents divorced a few years ago and his mother and the kids moved in with her father. Saturday morning the father showed up at the house to pick up the kids for a weekend visitation and the grandfather pulled out a gun because he hadn't paid child support in months. The father took a step forward and the grandfather shot him. He's claiming self-defense. Then that same evening Henry Hinn's father saw his ex-wife out on a date with another man. He wasn't very happy about it and shot the guy."

"What about Jenny Moore's house burning down?"

"That was just a random accident. That could have happened to anyone," added Mrs. Heath-Jolly, the school secretary.

Every day was a constant reminder of how sheltered my life had been. I was raised in a nice middle-class neighborhood where things like that did not happen.

Halloween was just around the corner. I was curious about what the other teachers planned to do about it. One day at the teacher's table in the cafeteria, I mentioned thinking of buying Halloween candy for my class.

"The upper grades don't celebrate that here," said Mrs.

Allred.

"Three or four years ago on Halloween night one of our sixth graders was found in a cemetery tied to a tree by some high school kids claiming to be devil worshipers," explained Mrs. Sirota. "The lower grades still celebrate it but only with jack-o-lanterns and clowns. No ghosts, skeletons, and demons allowed."

"Well that's certainly a mood killer."

My red (high) reading group finished **Bunnicula** and started **Charlie and the Chocolate Factory**. Instead of focusing on word-attack skills and comprehension, I tried to have students focus on setting, character, and plot. Many teachers like students to be able to predict what happens next in the story. I think stories are less interesting if I know what happens next. What is the point of reading it if you already know what will happen?

Perched on my tall director's chair, I caught a glimpse of a note being passed around. I casually stood up and began to meander around the room, starting well away from the note as if I had not noticed.

Approaching slowing from behind, I quickly snatched it

out of a girl's hand. She cringed and slumped down in her seat.

The note said:

9:20 Everyone cough

9:25 Everyone clear their throat

9:30 Everyone sneeze

I read the note out loud and said, "Well, this looks fun, let's do it."

At 9:20, I told everyone to cough. "Oh come on, that was a little weak. Try it again."

At 9:25 I told everyone to clear their throat. At 9:30 everyone sneezed.

"Boy that was fun wasn't it?"

Silence

"Ha ha ha, I'm still laughing," I said in the most serious expression I could muster. "George, do you think I should send for the school nurse, because it sounds like my class has pneumonia?"

"No sir."

I did not hear a peep from my class the rest of the period. I was proud of the way I handled that and thought I was finally getting a grip on this teacher thing.

Unfortunately, that feeling did not last long.

The office informed me that Earl Copeland, my most challenging student, would be out of school for a few days. He was in the hospital with broken ribs.

My students claimed to know all about it and told an elaborate story about someone breaking into the Copeland's home, and Earl was hurt trying to protect his mother from an invading rapist. A few days later I learned the truth, Earl's older brother hit him in the side with a wooden 2X4.

When Earl return to school about two weeks later, he was in a foul mood. He snarled and grumbled a few times during math class, but we got through it. Then we returned to our homeroom for the next class.

"Open your spelling books to page 83 and take out a blank sheet of paper. Always remember that your first and last name should be the first mark on your paper."

Earl got up and walked over to an absent student's desk. He reached in and pulled a sheet of paper out of the kid's notebook.

"Hey, stop!" I called out. "You can't take somebody else's property."

"You can't tell me what to do motherfucker!"

The students gasped as every eye in the room turned to me to see what I was going to do about it. I was wondering that too.

"Get out of my classroom!" was the best I could come up with. I put my hand on his arm and guided him out the door.

We walked downstairs and saw the principal standing in the hallway.

Mr. Ackley told Earl to go into his office while I explained what happened.

"This isn't the first time that something like this has happened with Earl. You were right to order him to leave, but you shouldn't have grabbed his arm."

"I had to get him away from the other kids. I didn't hurt him."

"That doesn't matter. You're not allowed to touch a student in a show of force. If a student refuses to leave, you're supposed to send for me. I won't touch him either. I'll order him to leave and if he still refuses, we call the police, but we, literally, don't take things into our own hands. Now go back to class and don't discuss it with the other students. Just pretend nothing happened."

Another lesson learned. So much for me feeling like I was getting a grip on this teaching thing.

That same afternoon, while my students were outside for P.E., I was grading and recording writing assignments in the grade book. I thought Kathy Brunner's paper sounded very familiar but was still partially distracted by the Earl Copeland mess. I went to enter the grade and noticed there was already a grade by Kathy's name for that assignment. I finished grading the rest of the papers and noticed that I had recorded a grade for everyone but Blaine Osteen.

I picked up the students and as we walked back to the classroom, I asked Blaine, "I didn't see a writing paper with your name on it. Is this your paper?"

"Yeah, that's my handwriting."

"It's a very good paper, one of your best, but would you mind telling me why you put Kathy's name on it?"

His eyes suddenly widened. Blaine knew he had been caught. His face morphed into a guilty grin.

Social studies was my favorite subject. We briefly covered Native Americans and European explorers and focused on the British colonies in America. Besides readings from the textbook, students were divided into small groups and each group made an oral presentation on one of the thirteen colonies.

Our colonial unit culminated with Colonial Day. Students were encouraged to dress in colonial clothes and we teachers rented colonial outfits from a costume shop. The cafeteria planned a special lunch that day: chicken, corn on the cob, soup beans, cornbread, and apple crumble.

Dressed like Benjamin Franklin, and with the help of a hot plate, onion skins, blue berries, and beets, I demonstrated how people dyed cloth in Colonial Times. Other fifth grade teachers taught candle dipping, tin crafting, and weaving as students rotated to all four classrooms.

The local newspaper sent out a photographer and published two pictures. The principal loved that.

A few days later we received a reply from Buckingham Palace. The small envelope contained a folded notecard saying the Queen had seen our letters and had commanded her Lady-in-Waiting to reply to us and express her thanks that we took the time to write to her. The Queen regretted not being able to send a picture of herself as it is her policy not to send pictures to anyone she has not met.

I read it to the class and stapled it to the bulletin board for all to see. For months, students quietly went up to it and stared, touching it just to make sure it was real.

All holidays are not equally appreciated. My favorites were Thanksgiving, Christmas, and birthdays. I know birthdays are not official holidays, but my family always made a big deal over birthdays. At school it was common for parents to bring in cupcakes or donuts on their child's birthday. I was warned to call it a 'celebration' and never a birthday party, because the faculty handbook said we were only allowed to have two parties a year, Christmas and End-of-the-Year. Yes, I agree that it sounds petty, but that is how bureaucracies work.

Thanksgiving break was here and Christmas was not far away. I still was not sure how we would celebrate it at school.

My grandfather, whom I was named after, suggested asking for a dollar or two from each student, and taking two or three students to the grocery store and letting them buy whatever they wanted.

"It will show them what it's like to shop with a budget," he said.

I loved his idea.

"Don't forget to bring a calculator, so they can add everything up BEFORE they get to the cash register," added my mother.

To be fair, I asked everyone in the room interested in shopping for our Christmas party to put their name in a box. The shortest student in the room pulled out three names.

The shortest, tallest, shyest, and smartest students in the room are often targets of ridicule. I tried to single them out for something positive.

"OK, if you bring me signed permission notes from your parents, we'll go to the grocery store right after school the day before our party."

The three students were excited when we arrived at Publix, but that changed quickly when they realized they only had a set amount of money to spend.

"Why don't you start with paper plates and cups?"

They quickly decided they didn't need plates because they could use the paper towels already in our classroom.

Then priorities came into play. They could either buy the more delicious Item A, or the less expensive Items B *and* C. Which would give them the best choice for their money? After changing their minds several times, the students finally agreed on what they wanted.

The food was put into the trunk of my car and I brought it to school the next morning.

Not much learning goes on the day before Christmas break. Teachers rely on word-search papers, crossword puzzles, and other fun activities in the morning. The parties begin after lunch.

If smiles were any indication, the party was a great success. Some students moved their desks into clusters and others sat in groups on the floor. They happily spent the afternoon talking, laughing, eating, and listening to music.

I had completely forgotten about students giving their teacher a gift and was flattered when about half of them placed a Christmas present on my desk.

When all the gifts were open, I had six bottles of cheap drug store cologne, seven ceramic mugs, three batches of homemade cookies, one box of chocolate covered cherries, a bottle of whisky from a student whose mother was a barmaid, and one apple with a missing bite. Altogether, not a bad haul for someone not expecting anything.

Being a beginning teacher was a lot like a poor swimmer trying to tread water. I was working as hard as I could just to keep my head above water. Now with a two-week Christmas break, I finally had a chance to see how far I was from the shore.

I was there trying to help the students, but, with the exception of the ones in the red (high) group, too many had the attitude that teachers, adults in general, were the enemy. They tended to resist whatever we were trying to teach. It was not just my class, I noticed that same tensions in other teachers' classes as well.

I also learned the importance of regulating my liquid intake. In most schools it is not considered professional to announce, 'I'll be right back, Teacher has to go potty.' On more than one occasion I held it in so long I thought my eyes were going to float away. Although it never actually happened, there were a few times when I felt like shoving kids out of the way so I could make it to the teachers' restroom in time.

As I took the roll the first day back from a break that flew by much too quickly, the principal came to my door.

"Mr. Williams, can you come over here? This is Manuel Martinez from Costa Rica, and he's going to be in your class. He doesn't speak any English so you're going to have to help him with everything. This is his sister," pointing to an attractive woman who appeared to be in her early twenties, "and her new husband. He was born here in Florida and is bilingual so he can help you with any language problems." He appeared to be at least a decade older than his young wife.

Students coming and going happened more frequently than I ever expected. Manuel brought my class up to forty students. I had to put him at a table until the custodian brought in another desk. Now I understood why my professors said to get friendly with the custodians and school secretary.

I tried to make Manuel comfortable, but it was obvious that he was ill at ease and uncomprehending. Luckily a few students spoke Spanish, so they helped him find the restroom and get through lunch.

On the way home from school I stopped at a bookstore and bought an English-Spanish dictionary and tried to learn a few basic words.

The next morning I greeted him at the door with, "Hola, Manuel. Bienvenido!" ("Hello, Manuel. Welcome!")

My accent may have been horrible, but his face lit up and his mood soared.

I also checked out a few Spanish books from the school library, all four of them, and put them at his seat.

I don't know if it was out of boredom or whether the books were actually that interesting, but they held his attention all morning.

I did not know the Spanish word for 'lunch,' so I pointed to my mouth and said, "El comer, el comer."

Manuel laughed out loud at my effort.

I thought I was saying 'eat' but was actually saying 'the eat, the eat.' From that point on he usually smiled whenever we made eye contract.

It was clear he was very intelligent, and Manuel could tell I was making an effort. He learned new English words much quicker than I learned Spanish words.

Manuel laughed way too hard when I said, "Maestro mucho inteligente" (teacher very intelligent) and "Maestro mucho hermoso." I thought the last one meant 'teacher very handsome' but I was actually saying 'teacher very beautiful.'

At first he was useless with word problems but if the math problems were written in numerals, Manuel could solve a page of them quicker than any student in the room.

The other kids loved hearing him laugh and would often tickle him. He quickly learned to say, "No more theese, no more theese!"

Manuel followed me around like a little puppy and acted like I was his best friend. Teachers are supposed to like all of their students equally. I always had trouble doing that, but consciously tried not to show it. How could I not like students who considered me their favorite?

As much as I enjoyed working with a student who was both eager to learn and appreciative, I had other students to attend to.

How can I best describe Oliver Bakker? Even though he had gone to Kenwood since kindergarten, he did not quite fit in and knew it. He always seemed to have the look of a frightened animal with shifty eyes looking for a quick way to escape. Oliver was slightly taller than average, physically awkward, and had brown hair with a close-cropped buzz cut. He did not appear to have any friends, struggled academically, and was pulled out once a week for counseling. Other teachers told me Oliver was a mechanical wizard who hunted through people's trash to find discarded equipment and could repair almost anything.

I still have no idea what triggered it but one day, just before lunch, Oliver had a meltdown. He stood up and yelled threats about bombing the school and bringing a gun to shoot people.

"Oliver, I think you need to cool down. Melissa and Travis, would you please escort him to the office to see the guidance counselor?"

He was not in school for the next few days. When he did come back, his demeanor was exactly the same, but there were no more outbursts.

I found a note in my office mailbox from Mr. Ackley, the principal, informing me of a parent conference before school the next morning in his office. All I could think about was, what had I done wrong?

Mr. Ackley sat on one side of his desk, and Mrs. Davisson, Mrs. Johnson, and I sat on the other. As a beginning teacher I mostly kept my mouth shut and listened. The mother wanted her twin sons put into the same class instead of different classes.

"Your sons get into a lot less trouble when they are not together. When they're together on the playground or cafeteria they tend to get into fights."

"If they're in the same room they would be able to help each other with their schoolwork. Wouldn't that be a good thing?"

"Mrs. Davisson, I hate saying this to a parent," explained the principal, "but your sons are aggressive. They bully and pick on other kids when they're together."

"I'm proud of them for that. My boys aren't so good at schoolwork but they can stand up for themselves. Nobody pushes my sons around."

"I think keeping them in separate classes is for the best."

"We'll see what you have to say when I go to the School Board about this."

I did not know it at the time, but experience has taught me that usually nothing comes from most of these threats.

It was my twenty-third birthday and I was not sure I had anything to celebrate. I wanted to become a teacher to make a difference in students' lives yet came home every day feeling as if I had done battle and most days did not feel like I had won. Did other teachers feel this way? My grandmother made chicken & dumplings for me and I pretended to feel happier than I actually felt. Was this really what being an adult was all about?

As we meandered into February, I had a new mission. Besides trying to get students to put their first and last names on their papers, I was determined to get them to say *Valentine's* Day, instead of Valentime's Day, and *library* instead of li*berry*.

"Mr. Williams," called Ricky Jeffries, pointing to Stacy Woodbury.

Stacy was walking back to her desk from the pencil sharpener and suddenly stopped, staring blankly into space. This was not the first time that had happened with her.

I quickly wrote down what happened and said, "Ricky, can you please take Stacy to the clinic? Give this paper to the nurse?"

A few minutes after the dismissal bell, the principal walked into my room to let me know what happened.

"I phoned Stacy's mother and suggested she take her to the doctor. She didn't sound at all concerned and said it had happened before. She didn't have a car, so she said Stacy could just take the bus home. I told her I would pick her up and we could both take Stacy to the doctor. She still wasn't interested but didn't object. You'll never believe what I saw out there. I saw it and still don't believe it. Mr. Woodbury lost his job so he raises bees to sell the honey. It's spring so he's moved a few hives into their house in hopes of keeping the bees from swarming. Bees were flying in and out of an open window. The doctor wasn't sure but thought Stacy had been stung in her ear and the swollen nerve was causing the problem."

"Is she going to be out of school for a few days?"

"No, school's the safest place for that girl."

Stacy was still having those spells two weeks later so was taken back to the doctor.

Again the principal came back to my classroom, "The test results have come back and now the doctor thinks Stacy's having petite mal seizures. It's a mild form of epilepsy and he's running more tests to confirm it. I found out that Stacy and her brother were adopted because their birth parents were abusing them. They would shut them in a closet and not feed them. That's why they overeat and sometimes hunt for food in garbage cans. I don't know if the state is going to let them stay in that home or not, but at least they'll be supervised."

This was just another reason to question whether my work was making any difference at all.

When my class returned to our room after lunch, I asked whether they would rather read the social studies textbook or hear me talk. They chose the lecture. I was sure that would be the case since listening takes less effort.

"In January of 1848, at Sutter's Mill in California, someone saw something sparkly in the water. It was a piece of gold about the size of a green pea. Word spread and by 1849, thousands and thousands of men came to California hoping to find gold and strike it rich. They lived in tents and shacks because new homes couldn't be built fast enough, and most of these men couldn't afford them anyway. The prospectors were called the forty-niners because they came in 1849. There were so many of them that they were getting in each other's way and there were a lot of fights. There was also a racial element. A heavy tax was put on foreign miners, especially on South Americans and the Chinese. A few of these miners did get rich, but most did not. A lot of money was made by merchants who sold supplies to the miners. The Chinese, who couldn't afford the heavy tax, were smart enough to know the miners needed to eat, so opened Chinese restaurants. When the gold rush was over many of the miners went back to where they came from and took their taste for Chinese food with them. That's why there are so many Chinese restaurants all over the place. I don't know about you, but I love Chinese food. Mining is rough work, so the miners were always ripping their pants. Jacob Davis came up with the idea of making rugged pants out of denim, and Levi Strauss owned a factory that started making them. Both guys became rich in the gold rush, but it was not because they found gold. Today those rugged pants are called blue jeans or Levi's."

Manuel's hand popped up and he blurted out, "I Levi's aqui."

I called him up and had him stand on a table in front of the room.

He stood there beaming as I explained, "These are the very pants I'm talking about. I know a lot of people think history is boring, but I think it's important to know why the world is the way it is. I don't think Chinese food or blue jeans would be nearly as popular as they are if it hadn't been for the California gold rush. Yes, something that far away and that long ago effects the way we live today. OK, the clock says it's time to pack your backpacks and get ready to go home."

The bus riders' bell rang five minutes before the final dismissal bell to give them a slight head start. That day some of my bus riders came back to the classroom to look at me and run out again, only to return one more time before finally leaving.

The next day they explained that their substitute bus driver looked just like me and they were trying to figure out how I was getting back and forth between the bus and classroom so fast.

I told that to my grandparents and they told me that one day they thought they saw me walking along a road and pulled the car over to ask why I wasn't in school before realizing it was not me.

While I enjoyed teaching about weather, plants, solar system, and vertebrates in science, social studies was always my favorite subject. I was not really interested in political or military leaders, but was fascinated by people who effected the culture.

For the last assignment of the school year, I gave the class a list of Influential Americans and told them to pick one and write a one-page report about that person.

"Pick anyone you like, but every good Floridian should know who Willis Carrier is."

Influential Americans

Julia Child
Elisha Otis
Thomas Edison
Henry Ford
Wilber & Orville Wright
Clarence Birdseye
Teressa Bellissimo
Harland Sanders
Jonas Salk
Percy Spencer
Orville Redenbacher
Willis Haviland Carrier
Ruth Wakefield
George Crum
Richard & Maurice McDonald
Jim & Peter Delmonico
Henry John Heinz
Noah Webster
Walt Disney

Garrett Morgan
Philo T. Farnsworth

1. Birth, Childhood, Education
2. What significant thing did he/she do?
3. How did it change people's lives?
   List 3 sources of information you used.

     The last assignment had been graded and the scores had

been recorded, analyzed, and stored. Report cards had been

handed out and the end-of-the-year party was coming to an end.

The final dismissal bell rang and most kids rushed out the door.

A few stopped to give me a hug and told me they would miss me.

I very much appreciated that. The room quickly emptied, and I

sat alone at my desk enjoying the silence.

     This whole year had been a huge learning experience for

me. I believe my professors meant well but most did not have

actual classroom experience and did not teach many of the things

I actually needed. Teaching has its own jargon of terms and an

alphabet soup of acronyms: IEP (Individual Educational Plan),

IPDP (Individual Professional Development Plan, pronounced

Ippy-Dippy), ESOL (English for Speakers of Other Languages), RTI (Response To Intervention), ADD (Attention Deficit Disorder, ADHD (Attention Deficit Hyperactivity Disorder, and many many more.

I was reminded of a story about two friends walking along the beach in the morning after a storm where hundreds and hundreds of starfish were washed ashore. One man picked up a starfish and threw it back into the water.

"What are you doing that for? There's too many here, that won't make a very big difference," said one friend.

"It'll make a big difference to this one."

OK, I won't be able to save the world, I cannot even save my whole class, but maybe if I can just make a difference for a few of them, the struggle and frustrations might be worth it.

TWO

I encouraged the students to use the question box (comment box) for things they wanted to ask or tell me in confidence. Reading some of the non-personal notes out loud encouraged the class clowns who wanted to see if I had the courage to read their notes. This sample of real students notes gives an insight into the fifth grade mind.

Would you move me somewhere else because Donna talks to me all the time and I can't do my work.

I love someone but no one knows who!

Mr. Williams, whenever you went to the beach did you see anyone streak?
Sam didn't write this

Mr. Williams is fantastic!

Tell Robert not to tell anyone else that I like Johnny because I hate him very much.

Mr. Williams,
I hate you, but don't ask who wrote this.

I think you have been a nice teacher, Mr. Williams.
When you tell us to be quiet you are doing it to be strict,
Mr. Williams. I am glad I am in your room.

Mr. Williams, how did Terry get to be so

ugly?

Mr. Williams,
I think you are 2,000,000 years old and you
weigh about 3,000,000 pounds and in the
waist you are 85 feet around.

Are you a baboon? You look like a pig.
You are a punk.

Are you going to teach next year? I want
you to tell me now.

Why don't you get married? You are too
ugly, and I right?

Mr. Williams is number 1, and that's as
high as I can count.

You look very cute.
Signed Henry

Mr. Williams is a wonderful man. I love you, I love you, but I tell lies.

Are photons solid, and if so, why doesn't gravity have any effect on them?

Roses are red, the stems are green,
Mr. Williams is cute, but gosh how mean.
By an admirer
P.S. Don't tell my teddy bear, because
he won't sleep with me tonight.

People are people, boys are keen
You have a figure like a submarine!
Signed Tugboat

IF a baboon would look at Joan, would it run or faint?

Don't look now but there is a monster liver

standing behind you!

Do you know that Johnny R. likes Paula B?
Yes or No?

When you get married don't marry a fool,
marry someone from Kenwood School.
Signed Paperweight

Please tease me more!

If I come to this school, I want you to be
my teacher.
Signed Your Pupil

Roses are red, trashcans are dirty,
You look like a little stinking birdie!
Signed Vulture

Mr. Williams,
Do you streak when you are home alone?

Do you sleep with your teddy bear?

Do you have a phone? What is your number?

Mr. Williams,
You are very very very very very very very very very very very very nice, wonderful, and great!
Signed You Stink!

Roses are red, violets are blue,
Everyone stinks, even you!

I hope you have a good class next year. You are a nice teacher but I don't think the kids like writing all the reports. I hope you have a nice summer.

Mr. Williams is eating his underwear because it is Fruit of the Loom!

Mr. Williams,

I bet I can make you turn this upside down!!!!

You should fail everyone who doesn't like you, that means you should fail: Tom, Jim Scott, Pete, and Rick.
From: Guess Who???

Don't read out loud!
Would you please kid around with me more?
When you finish, throw this note away.

Only a dunce would read this note!

I love you!

What do you do when you are of out school? This is not a nasty letter.

Dear Mr. Williams,

You might as well sit down and relax because this is going to be long. You see I'm really a girl deep deep down inside, but when I was in the 3rd grade I got the reputation of acting like a boy. Well, I still act like one, but I do like the attention I get when I act like a girl and wear dresses. If I wore one all the time, then I wouldn't get anything when I wore one because it would be common. I just wanted to let you know that I enjoy being a girl.

Two girls love me and I'm going to with one of them. What should I do?

Signed Private

Happy Valentine's Day.
From: Athena, Goddess of Wisdom

Are you sexy with your girls?

Mr. Williams,
How can you stand to listen to that
classical music junk?
Signed Somebody

Dear Mr. Williams,
You are so nice, I want to go home with
you and be your little girl. Then I could
know more about Greece and you could
answer all my questions. And I know you
are very strict.
Don't read my name!!!!!!!!!

Mr. Williams is a nice guy,
He's not very mean.
Some people think he is stupid,
I think he is keen.
When you're in his class
You know you can do his work,
But he really gets indignant
If you stand up and burp.
Some people think he's smart,
Some people think he's not.

I think he's a genius,
But I really lie a lot!!!!!!!

Humpty Dumpty sat on a wall,
Humpty Dumpty had a great fall.
All the king's horses and all the king's men
Had scrambled eggs.

Mr. Williams,
If you could be anyone in the world who
would you be?

I'm glad you don't wear short sleeves often
because your arms are so hairy you look
like an ape.

Why do people write dumb notes?

Don't read this note out loud, just say yes
or no after you read it. Do you ever look at
Playboy Magazine? (Say yes or no)

Mr. Williams,
I don't know how you can stand up all day.
My bones would be killing me.

Mr. Williams,
If you have any other kind of shoes
PLEASE WEAR THEM!!!!!

How come we have 17 Gertrudes and 14
Freds in our class?

Mr. Williams,
If you believe it or not, roses are red,
violets are blue, and if you don't believe
me, you are weird and I'm going to break
your nose!!!!

Roses are red, violets are blue,
Lend me ten dollars and I'll love you.

Mr. Williams,

Whenever you read those funny notes, you look at me like I wrote them. Well I didn't, except for this one.
P.S. Do your impression of Jimmy Carter

Mr. Williams,
Please tell Bobby to stop peeing in the sink.

What would you do if you had bad grades?

Do you like your job?

Only a dummy would unfold this note.

Mr. Williams,
Please tease me more.

Mr. Williams,
Please throw this paper away for me!

Mr. Williams,
Your eyes are like the sky, they are so blue,
Your hair is like wild fire, it is so wild,
Your ears are so big, and your hands so
soft, and your shoes so UGLY!!!!!!

Mr. Williams,
I think you are the nicest person in the
whole world. Now can I have an 'A'?

Mr. Williams,
When you were born they found the
definition for the word terror!

Don't look behind you, there is a mirror
and we don't want you to faint.

Roses are red, grass is green,
You have a shape like a washing machine.

Get some new shoes!!!!!!!!!!!!

Mr. Williams,
    After you get through reading this note,
would you please go on to the next one.

Mr. Williams,
    You're so mean when you were a
student you kept your teachers after school.

Mr. Williams,
        Please tease me a lot more.

Mr. Williams,
    When you were born I'll bet you slapped
                the doctor!

Mr. Williams,
    You love yourself, you think your grand,
    You go to the movies and hold your hand.
    You put your arm around your waist,
    And if you get fresh you slap your face.

Mr. Williams,
You are a very nice guy when you give me a good grade, but when you give me a bad one, you don't know how mad I be.

Why do you always tease George? Tease me too!

This note will self-destruct in ten seconds!!!!!!

THREE

Florida schools usually start a week or two before Labor Day. Most people think that teachers have it easy because we get two months off in the summer, two weeks off at Christmas, and one week off in spring. Actually that is pretty good, but what they do not know is that our contracts are only for ten months. We are unemployed over summer breaks, so we do not get paid. Most school boards give teachers the option of having money withheld during school year and then give us our own money over the summers. Summers are NOT paid vacations.

I was accepted into graduate school at Rollins College and spent the summer taking two classes that could lead to a master's degree in Administration/Supervision K-12.

The teachers and staff gathered in the cafeteria the first morning of pre-planning week. It was nice to see familiar faces again. I still had a lot more to learn, but I knew a lot more than I did last year.

I had no idea how significant it would become, but one of many boring items the principal told us about was, "The State of Florida and our local school board are making an effort to synchronize and unify the curriculum. They've produced a guide for every one of you that enumerates specific skills for each grade level in each subject, suggestions for teaching each skill, and the month they would like it to be taught. They are also supplying blank graphs to plot your class's progress, and folders to keep student papers showing they've mastered each skill."

Groans came from all around me.

"This year it's optional, but it will become mandatory one day. Like it or not, this is the future because the state legislature is demanding accountability."

I had to keep reminding myself that diamonds are formed under extreme pressure.

The rest of pre-planning week went smoothly. I went out to lunch every day because I knew it would be a long time before I could do that again on a weekday.

Mr. Montgomery's comment about the school lunch being tasty only if you liked the taste of sawdust turned out to be overly generous.

Last year I was nervous about Meet Your Teacher Day because I did not know what to expect. This year I was nervous because I *did* know what to expect. Again, just like last year, parents were more interested in talking to each other than in meeting their child's teacher, me. The apple doesn't fall far from the tree. A few of my students from last year dropped in to say 'hi.' That was easily the highlight of my week.

Returning to school after summer break disrupts their routines so students are usually dazed and on their best behavior for the first few days. By the third or fourth day, reality rears its ugly head.

One of my students impressed me as the quietest kid ever seen. She never said a word. Even when you asked her a direct question she would just nod or shrug. At first I thought she was extremely shy and gave her a little space, but soon noticed a vacant look in her eyes.

When her permanent record arrived from her old school - yes, permanent records are real - I learned she had an IQ of 50. IQs between 85 and 115 are considered normal. IQs 70 or below are considered retarded. An IQ of 50 is very low. We had special classes for people like her, but her father was too proud to admit that she had a problem and refused to sign the admission forms. I did the best I could for her, but it was not nearly enough.

After two weeks in our homeroom groups we began to change classes for reading and math.

I stood before my class, hoping to spark their interest.

"I know this is a reading class but we're going to begin with a writing assignment. Some words like supercalifragilisticexpialidocious are just sounds put together that don't mean anything. But the sounds in some words do have meaning. For example, 'photo' means light, and 'graphy' means to draw or write. Put them together photo-graphy or photography, and it means to draw or write with light. 'Bio' means life, as in biology, the study of living things. So what does bio-graphy or biography mean?"

"To write about life?" suggested one student.

"Yes, to write about someone's life. Now 'mobile' means move and 'auto' means self, so auto-mobile means something that can move itself. OK, now let's put three of those together. What does auto-bio-graphy or autobiography mean?"

"To write about yourself," offered another student.

"Oh, you guys are brilliant! That's exactly right. I've written my autobiography and I want to hear what you think of it. Here goes…....

Brenford Williams

I was born at an extremely young age. I was so young that twenty-four hours after I was born, I was only one day old. I did not speak or write very well, but I did cry a lot. A day went by, then another, and still another. Three hundred and sixty-five days after my birth, I had my first birthday. I was around one-year-old at the time. A few more birthdays came and I noticed that my age changed each time. I guess that is what makes me special. I always knew I was very bright because my parents called me sun, or was that son? I always get those two confused. Over the years I did a lot of stuff, visited a lot of places, and met a lot of people. Sometimes I can even remember some of them. Since then I have had several more birthdays and, can you believe it, each time my age changed again. That is the story of my life up until today when I wrote this story. I am sorry I do not have a better ending for this story because the truth is, I do not know how it ends. I do not even know when it will end. I just hope it has a happy ending. Actually, I think this story is so interesting that I hope it never ends. Perhaps I should call this The NeverEnding Story. My life's goal is to live forever, so far so good!

What do you think of it?"

Some students nodded approval, most smiled, and some said it was very good.

"I'm glad you liked it. Perhaps you liked it because you think teachers are smart. Or perhaps you liked it because it was funny, but it was actually a very poor autobiography. It's supposed to tell you about me, and it does not tell you anything except that I'm male and still living. You already knew that before I read it. At least I hope you did. An autobiography should tell you about things I've done, things I liked, things I don't like, and things I think and dream about. Your assignment is to write a one-page autobiography. Things like your height, weight, and hair color can be part of it, but only a small part. When I read it, I want to know who you are on the inside."

I was genuinely interested in learning who my students were and laughed out loud when I read one boy's paper who wrote, 'My hand hurts from all this writing.'

I needed something fun, so signed up for a photography class for teachers at a local community college. The course was designed to instruct teachers how to make some of their own teaching materials.

Our first assignment was to make a slide presentation for our class in one of the subject areas and then share it with the photography class. I decided to make a creative writing assignment and told my students to make up ten completions for the phrase 'Happiness is......'. I selected the best of the ten from each student and had the students pose for my camera to illustrate them. I then recorded a soundtrack for the slide show.

Happiness is.........

......a new baseball glove

......a new doll

......getting an "A" on a spelling test

......a teacher's smile

......winning a fight with your big sister

......getting together with your friends

......knowing the right answer to your teacher's question

......getting to lick the bowl when your mother bakes a cake.

......a big muscle

......playing hide-and-go-seek

......when the teacher shows another movie

......walking barefoot in the grass

......hitting the ball on the first swing

......a chain of paperclips

......winning a blue ribbon

......sleeping in the backseat on the way home

......a new box of crayons

.......a warm sweater on a cold day

......all 'A's on your report card

.......the end of a long day

My students wanted to see the slideshow over and over again. It was a rare opportunity to see themselves in the spotlight for something good.

I remember my fifth grade teacher trying to teach nouns, verbs, adverbs, and adjectives. I also remember thinking, 'this is dumb, I don't need to know this garbage.' Trying to cram skills down my throat that I thought were pointless was a terrible approach. I believe creative writing assignments are a great way to teach writing skills. It allows students to explore and express their own ideas and helps turn them into independent thinkers. Reading their stories to the class makes them want to be better writers. They begin to see the point to proper word usage and proper punctuation. I gave writing topics such as:

Imagine our class is stranded on a deserted island.

If you could spend a day with anyone, who would you pick and

what would you do?

Describe the perfect vacation.

What is the happiest day you can imagine?

If you could be invisible for one day, what would you do?

A few of the more experienced teachers recommended
that I assign extra writing assignments as punishment for
students who talked too much in class. I tried but did not think it
was very effective. Students turned in papers on animals, trees,
states, countries, planets, and people. I don't think the students
ever expected them to be read.

School

By Melanie

*Sometimes I think school is a waste of time. First of all
the teachers give you all the stuff you learned last year. In some
classes, I know the teachers give us third grade work.*

I hate getting up at 7 o'clock. We have to go home at 3:15. Sometimes the bus is so slow I don't get home until 3:55.

We have to work all week to get ready for some tests with people we haven't even heard of on it.

The food is rotten. When we have hamburgers, they have little green things on them.

In some classes I know the teacher gives stupid reports all day. If you even ask a question above the yelling class, he'll give you a report just exactly like this one.

Sometimes we get so much work in school that I wish I could dig a hole and stick my head in it.

A President

George Washington was very famous. You notice I used 'was' because he died a long time ago. Lots of people liked him.

I am now doing a report on President Bush. The reason my report on Washington isn't long is because I wasn't born when he was alive, but I was alive when Bush was alive, so I will do a report on Bush.

Bush was a very bad president, hardly anyone liked him,
but some people did. I don't know why people hated him, and I
don't care.

Now I will do a real real real real long report on Ford.
Ford was a president. He has a name like the car, Ford, so if
you have a Ford car and always forget the name of a President,
go look at your car.

Our classroom had a long narrow closet or cloakroom,
but since we were in Florida there was rarely a need to hang
sweaters, jackets, or coats in there. The closet had a narrow
awning window with a broken latch. Even a slight breeze could
blow the window open. It was not really a problem until I started
finding bird droppings in the closet nearly every day. The birds
flew in after school and on weekends to building a nest. The
custodians moved the nest to a tree outside and filled out the
form to request maintenance to repair the window.

In Florida, school districts are county-wide and Kenwood
Elementary was in a large school district. Nothing gets done

without the proper paperwork and then you wait. A few weeks later a maintenance man came out from the county school board office, took one look at it and said it could not be fixed. It looked fairly simple to me, so I tied a rope to the lever and attached a weight. It looked sloppy but problem solved.

I sat down at the teachers' table in the cafeteria just in time to hear Mr. Montgomery say, "I swear that boy's a mental midget. If his brains were dynamite, he wouldn't have enough to blow his nose."

"In an effort to change the subject," said Mrs. Sirota turning toward me, "what do you think of the new accountability system, Mr. Williams?"

"You guys know a lot more about it than I do," I replied, "but it seems like a lot of extra work. All that record keeping takes time away from working with the kids. We'll each need our own secretary if we have to do all that."

"The skills in this thing range from putting punctuation at the end of a sentence to writing a report on the impact of television on people's political opinions," added one teacher.

"In social studies, students are supposed to make a list of

the characteristics of 'good citizenship' and explain why each item is important. Another skill requires the student to explain the changes of values in a culture," explained Mrs. Allred.

"Oh good god, I'm not sure I could do that," said Mrs. McCall.

"No wonder there's a teacher shortage," commented Mr. Montgomery.

I walked my class from the cafeteria to their weekly music class and, on the way back to my classroom, saw one of my last year's students in the hallway on the verge of tears.

"What's the matter, Alice?"

"Mr. Williams, I have to go home," as she clung to me in a big hug.

"Are you sick?"

"No," she wailed, "I have lice!"

My eyes popped wide open and every muscle in my body froze tightly. I was proud of myself for not shoving her aside and running away screaming. I took a step back, trying hard to show compassion, but all I could think of was stopping by a drug store on the way home from school to buy lice shampoo.

I returned to my classroom to find 'F__K' written on the chalkboard in large letters. That sort of thing was routine around here, so I erased it and moved on.

I picked up my students from music class and led them to the restrooms for a quick break. One of the students came out of the boys' room with a soggy foot.

"What happened?" I asked in surprise.

"I, well, I…"

He squirmed and clearly did not want to answer, but other boys eagerly jumped in.

"He was standing on the toilet seat and slipped."

"Ray was trying to look over the partition into the next stall."

"Oh good grief."

I wondered what other people did at their jobs.

Christmas break could not get here quick enough. This year I received eight bottles of cheap cologne and six more mugs. Mugs are fine for beginning teachers, but we very soon get swamped with them.

The school board offered a central film library where

teachers could order movies to show in their classrooms. I ordered seven films and filled out the papers to have one arrive each week. Someone at the school board office must have had a sadistic sense of humor because they all arrived the same day and were all due back in one week. I borrowed a movie projector from our school library and began showing a movie marathon. For two days, other teachers refereed to me as Cecil B. DeWilliams and my classroom as the Metro-Goldwyn-Williams Theater. If I ever leave teaching, I am an experienced movie projectionist.

To say my desk was a bit cluttered is a fair comment, and it could even be considered a bit of an understatement. I tolerated it because I could find whatever I was looking for in under five minutes. One day I tried to find my grade book but it was missing. When it still had not turned up by the next day, I told the principal about it. He was not happy but took the news better than I expected. I offered the students a ten-dollar reward to whoever returned it, no questions asked.

The next morning my grade book was returned by a girl named Precious Robertson.

"I was at my friend's house yesterday and saw that she had it. I took it from her when she wasn't looking because I knew it was yours."

Everything was just as I had left it except all of Precious' grades had miraculously changed to A's.

The principal called her parents to come in for a conference. I hated parent-conferences dealing with behavior issues. Parents are defensive and often become so obnoxious that I leave wondering how the kid turned out as well as he or she did. This conference was especially eye-opening.

I learned that Precious's parents were divorced, and her mother married her former father-in-law, her ex-husband's father. Precious's mother was also her step-grandmother and her ex-husband's stepmother. Precious's father was now her stepbrother. Someone figured out that Precious was now both her own aunt and niece.

I wanted things to get back to normal, as if anything in this job was normal.

I assigned the red reading group to read a play and write a one-page critique. The next step was to write an original play of their own, five to ten minutes long, AND they would act them out in class.

As always, some kids handed in their papers early. Most came in on time, and there were always a few stragglers who turned their assignments in late or not at all.

I read them as they were turned in and called Stacia LeMasters aside.

"You did the assignment, but you're going to have to fix it if you want to act it out in front of the class."

"Why? I asked you if I could write about a boy who stole something and learned his lesson."

"Yes you did, but you didn't mention anything about him stealing a laxative and getting diarrhea. I don't think that's appropriate for a fifth grade play. You did the assignment, so I'll give you the grade, but you need to change it if you want to act it out."

"That's not fair! I asked you about it and you said it was OK."

Her play was about a boy who stole a package of Ex-Lax because it looked like chocolate. When he feared getting caught before he could leave the drug store, he swallowed the evidence and then messed his pants.

The next morning the girl's grandmother was in Mr. Ackley's office yelling about how unfair it was that I would not let Stacia act out her play after approving it.

I will never understand the way some people think.

The creativity of my students impressed me. A girl wrote about an airplane trip and acted it out by tossing a model plane across the room to another student. The weirdest play was called 'The Bionic Orange Peel.' The orange peel could fly and had super strength. The play began with a bank robbery which the kids acted out. The thieves drove away and accidentally drove off a bridge. Nick, the playwright, built a bridge out of books and his model car careened off the side, only to be scooped up by the orange peel and delivered to the police, making the world safe for democracy.

We even had our own version of the Tony Awards. 'The Bionic Orange Peel' won just about every category.

I encourage students to take notes when I teach but noticed one girl rapidly writing during one of my lessons, even during pauses. I slowly walked by and snatched the paper. I put it in my desk and did not look at it until after school.

I was shocked to find the most obscene letter I've ever seen. It was to a boy in my homeroom inviting him to get together after school to have sex AGAIN. According to the letter, the last time they did it was his first time, but not hers. She thought he was clumsy and wanted him to do better this time. Another girl would be there as a lookout.

I took it to the principal and he immediately called the mother of the girl who wrote it. The mother wanted him to read the letter over the phone. He said it was too embarrassing so he asked her to come to school so she could see it for herself. I later heard that the mother could not read so he had to read it to her face-to-face. I would have loved to be a picture hanging on the wall in his office when that happened.

The next afternoon, I stood in front of my social studies class and said, "As much as I enjoy studying about the American colonial times, I think I like studying the Constitution even more. Many adults are confused by the Constitution. I don't understand why, it's actually pretty simple. If you've ever helped your mother make biscuits, you follow a recipe. You mix flour, milk, butter, and a pinch of baking soda and a pinch of salt to form a dough. You roll it out, cut it into round shapes, and bake them in the oven. That is all the constitution is, a recipe for how the government works. It is not a law but tells us how laws are made and who makes them. It divides the government into three equal branches so no one person can control everything. The legislative branch makes the laws. The executive branch carries out the law. And the judicial branch decides what laws mean and whether a law has been broken or not. Then there is the Bill of Rights that give us freedom of speech and other rights."

I explained how each branch of the government worked and told the students to imagine that we were starting our own country and write down ten laws they thought we needed. Then I had the class act out how a bill was passed and became a law. Finally, I had the students write their own constitution for our imaginary country.

My favorite one, written by a student named Jack Mavrides.

We, the kids of Juvenilia, hereby declare that we are free of baths, soap, spinach, carrots, and grownups. We have earned this right through the three-day war using only our hands, teeth, slingshots, BB guns, and our killer animals Big Bird, Freddy Frog, and Underdog.

ARTICLE 1 Human Rights

We declare when you reach the age of 10, or pass the second grade (whichever comes first *), you have the right to marry, get a car, and eat an adult portion of food. We further declare that being of mature mentality, no one can tell you what to do. Old folks can no longer push us around.
* (for our slow people)

ARTICLE 2 National Defense

An army shall be raised for the defense of our beloved nation, Juvenilia, who in time of hostilities by enemy nations, or by internal enemies (juvenile delinquents) must have the ability to win all battles on land, in trees, on rooftops, and in lakes (navy).

Weapons maintained in the arsenal must include the latest design of slingshots, spit-ball throwers, water pistols, and full equipment for all tree forts.

ARTICLE 3 Governing Bodies

The three branches of government are as follows:

(A) Executive – The person in charge of this branch of the Government shall be known as the Big Kid. All following Big Kids shall be elected by popular vote.

(B) Law Passing Branch – This branch of government shall be elected by popular vote, to serve a term of two weeks.
We have decided that a Senate is not needed since most Senators seem to be busy admiring themselves and planning to be the next Big Kid, and can't find the time to be good lawmakers.

(C) Judiciary – This branch of government shall be known as the Kangaroo Court. It shall have the power to interpret the constitution as its members see fit.

ARTICLE 4 Amendments

1. *Persons over the age of 25 must retire and are eligible for benefits for the aged.*

2. *No law shall be passed to govern the length of hair people wear.*

3. *Women shall be treated exactly the same as men, because at our age who can tell the difference these days?*

They were not all so brilliant. Here is another for comparison.

Constitution of the United Islands

Every man has his choice of religion, as long as it is Jewish.

Anyone who says anything against the government shall be punished. The citizens of the United Islands shall not be denied the right to vote. The Vice-president has to collect taxes from the rich, but not the poor. The President shall be the commander of the army and navy of the United Islands.

1. *You don't have to eat your vegetables when your mother tells you.*

2. *You don't have to go to school.*

3. *You can't wear your hair short-short or long-long.*

4. *No one but people over 70 have to work.*

5. *No one over the age of 15 can stay out past 5:00 P.M.*

6. *Children eat first.*

7. *Everybody must have brown hair and blue eyes.*

8. *No one can smoke alone.*

I saw a lot more of the inside of the principal office than I ever did my first year.

"I don't know what you're doing up there, but your social studies lessons are getting the kids all stirred up. I saw something about communism and fascism in your lesson plans. What's going on?" asked Mr. Ackley, looking mildly annoyed.

"I just wanted to do a brief introduction of capitalism, communism, fascism, and socialism so they would have a vague idea what they were if they ever heard it on the TV news. Why is something going on?"

"Is something going on," he said sarcastically. "First, these kids don't watch the news, but it's a good effort. You sure know how to get their attention. Second, they formed groups on the playground in the morning, calling themselves communists, capitalists, fascists, and socialists. Nothing has happened yet, but they're taunting each other. I don't want to see this turn into the 'Great Playground War.' See to it that your lesson today includes something about détente and peace treaties."

I decided to treat myself to a weekend in Sarasota. Besides beautiful beaches, it has the Ringling Museum, and St. Armands Circle for shopping and nice restaurants.

I returned to school in a better mood only to learn that Oliver Bakker, one of my students from last year, had drowned in a lake. He got tangled up in some of the weeds growing near the shore. I knew the answer was no, but I couldn't help wondering if there was anything more I could have done for him.

My college courses taught me what to teach and how to teach it, but did not tell me how to deal with students with emotional problems or who came from abusive homes or even how to deal with slow learners. They made it seem like all you had to do was let the special area teachers know and everything would be taken care of. I had no idea that it was so difficult to get students into those programs and how many parents refused to sign the admission papers because they did not want to admit that their child had a problem in the first place. Getting a student into those special programs usually began with testing and I heard about one school district that had no money for the tests. Those were only some of the problems that often made me feel like I walked around under a cloud of gloom.

My northern relatives made fun of me when I talked about Florida winters. We break out our long-sleeves and sweaters when the temperature dips into the 60s and break out our heavy coats when it gets into the 50s. Cold days are so rare that some of our older houses do not even have heaters.

During our current cold spell I heard Jack Mavrides telling someone, "It's freezing out there, even the palm trees are shivering."

In math class, I heard a commotion coming from the far corner of the room. One of the girls had the reputation of being a tomboy. She usually dressed and acted like a boy. That day she tried to prove she was really a girl by unbuttoning her shirt and showing her bare chest. Unfortunately, there was very little evidence to support her case.

The next morning, I was called into the principal's office to be told I was getting a new student. Sylvia Tackett ran away from her home and after the police returned her, she attempted suicide. She was now staying in a foster home and still had the bandages on her wrists. Sylvia would be wearing long-sleeves to school to hide them. I was told she was not a behavior problem but cautioned to handle her with kid gloves.

Springtime arrived. Flowers bloomed, birds sang, and everyone was supposed to be happy. Whatever it was that was supposed to happen to people in the spring was not happening to me. I felt exhausted and depressed. One night I was feeling especially sorry for myself and wrote a letter to a friend in Baltimore.

Dear Natalie,

A few months ago you wrote to me saying you needed someone to talk to. Now it is my turn.

Everything seems to be dull and uninteresting, my job, my friends, my whole life. Sometimes I'd rather be anyone but me. I keep asking myself 'What is life all about?' I always keep coming up with the same answer, a big question mark. My life is empty, useless, and meaningless.

I live from one payday to another with nothing worthwhile in between. Four weeks to go.....three weeks to go....twelve days to go....five more days....and when payday finally gets here, the whole thing starts all over again.

A philosopher once said there were three things a person needs to be happy, something you enjoy doing, someone you love, and something to look forward to. One out of three is not a very good average.

I could enjoy teaching a lot more, but there are two big problems. Somewhere along the way the students here have the idea that all teachers are the enemy. Being an only child, I imagined my students would be like the nieces and nephews I never had. Boy was I naïve. It is actually only a handful of them, but they fight everything I try to do for them. They NEED help. Too many of them come from homes where they don't have money for shoes but do have money for beer. I don't understand the world they live in. It is a real culture shock and it's getting to me.

The other problem is all the red tape, paperwork, and supervision. We have all kinds of reports to fill out on what we are teaching and how we are teaching it. It is all just to prove to some bureaucrat that we are doing SOMETHING and not just twiddling our thumbs. They are even starting to micromanage what we teach and how to teach it. I thought I went to college to learn that for myself. I know my students better than anyone else knows them. I know what they have learned and what they have not learned. I am spending most of my time filling out reports to keep the principal, the school board, and the Department of Education happy. It's not helping me at all and takes away from time I need to spend with my students. I'm a teacher, not a miracle worker. That isn't what I want to do for the rest of my life.

In college I took a personal interest inventory and scored high in humanities and politics. The college counselor who gave me the test joked that I should be a dictator of a museum. I would like almost anything in the area of the arts: painting, acting, philosophy, or writing. The main problem is that you have to have talent and I don't. I may stand a chance as a writer because I think this is going to be a long letter. There would be plenty of meaning and satisfaction working in the arts. To entertain and to give people a chance to lose themselves in your work is a wonderful thing.

Politics would be interesting, but I don't even know how to get started. I also doubt people would support my ideas.

As for the second thing the philosopher said, someone to love, I seem to be left out there too. Sure I date, but so far I haven't found anyone I would want to spend the rest of my life with. I don't even have someone I can call a close friend. I have friends, but no close friends and there is a big difference. A friend is someone you like to do things with or share an interest with. A close friend is someone you just enjoy being with, you don't have to do anything. It is someone you can share your real feelings with. My friends are so caught up in their own rat race, they don't have time for anything else either.

As for something to look forward to, I'm always looking forward to summer vacation. Having summers off is pretty good.

I hope I haven't bored you too much with my problems. It feels a lot better just to tell someone how I feel.

Brenford

I woke up the next morning feeling much better about the world, and never mailed the letter.

I do not know whether my letter writing had anything to do with it, but when my class became too talkative, I *ordered* them to stop. I had reached the end of my rope. I did not know what I was going to do, and it might cause me to wind up in jail, but by god I knew they were going to stop, right now! And they did. Looking back on it, I cannot tell that I did anything differently that I had done in the past but something inside me had changed just like Mrs. Sirota said it would, and so did their behavior. Oh the kids were far from angels and didn't always behave, but there was a huge improvement after that point.

I was very flattered when the teachers elected me to represent our school at the Florida Education Association Convention in Miami. The FEA was the state level of the National Education Association. It was traditional for each teacher to donate a few dollars to help cover expenses of transportation, hotel room, and meals. Yes, I would have to pay the difference out my own pocket, but it also meant missing three days of school. My mother arranged for me to ride there and back with the teachers from her school. I only had to pay my share of the gas.

The music teacher collected the money for me and left it in my mailbox in the office. The next day there were two more dollars paper-clipped to a note that read,

Janet Allred is donating this extra two dollars for you to have a drink or some kind of fun in the 'big city.' She says you are NOT to go back to your room after the meetings and go to bed. HAVE SOME FUN!!!!

I put the note into a sealed envelope and wrote 'I found this in my mailbox' on the outside and handed it to a student to give to Mr. Montgomery.

A few minutes later a student handed me a sealed envelope. Inside was one dollar and a note that said,

This is for a nice-looking hooker who works cheap!!!

On the way down to Miami I learned that being selected to go to the convention was not really the honor I thought it was. It was something usually foisted on the new teachers because the older ones did not want to be bothered. The meetings were long and boring, they tended to avoid controversial topics, and the outcomes of most votes were already known ahead of time, the voting was just a mere formality. The hot topics of this year's convention were reducing class size and dealing with accountability.

Once back at school it seemed like the principal was giving me the cold shoulder. I mentioned it to a few other teachers and they thought he was giving them the same treatment. So far that school year, one teacher had been fired and three had applied to transfer out. I even heard that some parents started a petition to get rid of him, though I had no idea why.

I put my name on the transfer list in hopes of getting to a school closer to my home.

On the last day of school my students gave me a certificate saying:

This certifies that Brenford Williams is awarded this certificate at Kenwood School from the students of 5th grade for being the best teacher in the state of Florida.

We sincerely hope you like your certificate, and we hope you will be a very nice teacher as you are for years to come.

Keep up the good work

On the same day I was given another student-made certificate.

I began my summer vacation looking forward to a little boredom.

FOUR

Nearly every week I give the students six to eight vocabulary words for them to look up and copy the definitions, study those definitions, and take a test at the end of the week. It was easy to tell who studied that week and who had not.

Altitude – the way people feel about something.

Ambushed – what a Southerner says when he tired.

Apprentice – one who prints newspapers.

Aspiring – to sweat a lot.

Assault – something you put on your food.

Astray – where you put lit cigarettes.

Assembly – to put something together.

Bazaar – a piece of women's underwear.

B.C. – to be for Christ.

Burly – a kind of cereal.

Charter – a person who makes charts.

Charter – part of a book.

Climate – something you climb.

Communicable – germs that talk to each other.

Communist – a person who is not on our side.

Date – when you go out with your girlfriend.

Decomposer – a person who writes music.

Delta – an airplane company.

Dense – not very smart.

Debt – how far down you can go.

Discharge – to take away your credit card.

Edition – to total two or more numbers.

Elevation – a machine that moves people one floor to another.

Entitle – to name a book or song.

Fief – a person who steals your things.

Fiord – paper to wrap gifts with.

Friction – a story that isn't true.

Glacier – a great big ice cube.

Government – the place where all taxes go.

Guild – to lead the way through the woods.

Guild – a magazine, like the TV Guild, to show what's on TV.

Gulf – a place where you buy gasoline.

Heralded – to be named Harold.

Heredity – something you catch from your family.

Heretic – to receive after someone dies.

History – a book in school that helps you learn.

Hydroelectric – electric rain.

Instinct – a bird that don't exist no more.

Invasion – to ask someone to a party.

Irrigation – to make someone mad.

Jester – a person who rides jets.

Journeyman – a man who travels.

Kitchenette – a net that you use in the kitchen.

Liberty – a place where you can borrow books.

Meridian – what a physician studies in college.

Meridian – the name of a sea south of Europe.

Misdemeanor – a long word.

Mt. Olympus – the place where the Greeks made grease.

Mummy – a body raped to keep it from decaying.

Neuter – a person who goes naked.

Oasis – I don't know but Mr. Williams does.

Passport – a report that you a good grade for.

Peasant – a bird they used to eat in the old days.

Pilgrim – people who eat turkey.

Poland – the yellow powder from a flower.

Population – a place where you are popular.

Prescription – to order a magazine through the mail.

Protestant – a woman who has sexual relationships with men for money. (This was an actual vocabulary test answer by the principal's son.)

Persecuting – to decorate a purse.

Recreation – a place where you recreate.

Reserved – when you serve something and then have to serve it again.

Scandinavia – a type of religion.

Serf – you surf on a wave.

Sinkhole – the hole in a sink.

Splendor – he removed a splendor from my finger.

Stark – the bird that brings babies to people.

Terrain – like a long bus, but it's on a track.

Vassal – what you put flowers in.

Veterinarian – someone who fought in a war.

FIVE

Being on the transfer list was no guarantee of moving to a new school. I still had to be interviewed and approved by the new principal. I didn't know until I showed up for the interview, but the principal of Princsonia Elementary School, Mr. Adams, was my old physical education teacher from high school. I wasn't very athletic and the nicest thing he ever barked at me was, "Williams, get your butt moving!" He claimed to remember me but I'm not sure he really did. There was no reason for him to because I was a quiet kid who tried not to be noticed. Mr. Adams was impressed that I was working on my master's degree, plus male teachers were in short supply at the elementary level.

The trend of moving the sixth grade out of elementary schools into middle schools had not reached Princsonia Elementary yet, but the sixth grade was departmentalized just like in middle school. I was offered a sixth grade social studies position and accepted without hesitation.

The newer one-story school was more modern than Kenwood Elementary. For example, Kenwood had a row of windows going across the whole outer wall of each classroom. At Princsonia there were two narrow windows going from floor to ceiling. The new school was air-conditioned and had a small restroom in each class.

This was my third pre-planning week, so I knew what to expect. There were five sixth grade teachers. One taught reading, one math, another language arts, the fourth was a science teacher. I would be the social studies teacher. My subject was a compilation of history, geography, civics, and economics, with a pinch of political science, sociology, anthropology, and maybe even a touch of psychology.

The evening before the students' first day, I wrote a letter to a friend in Baltimore.

Dear Natalie,

Tomorrow I have to face a group of sixth graders who have just had their summer vacation end by a school bell. I don't like it any better than they do. It's hard to like anything that gets me out of bed at six o'clock in the morning.

I took two more graduate level courses over the summer. Those plus the other graduate classes I've taken put me near the halfway point toward being the first in my family to get a master's degree. One of my professor's favorite sayings was 'reach one, teach one,' meaning if we only make a difference in one student's life, we'd be doing a good job. That plus accepting my limits that a teacher can only do so much, makes me go into this school year with new hope.

On the first day of school it was obvious that my students were cleaner and much better dressed than those at Kenwood. The day went smoothly until the bus bell rang.

One of my students asked me to bend down so she could

whisper something in my ear. When I did, Elizabeth gave me a quick kiss on my cheek and ran out the door leaving me visibly surprised and my class roaring with laughter.

Three days later she wrote me a letter saying she wanted to come to my house to cook and clean for me.

I took the note home to brag to my family how much my students liked me.

"If she's any good at cooking and cleaning, you need to keep an eye on this one," said my grandmother. "She won't be eleven forever."

I thought my grandmother was joking but later learned that she was not. She was raised in the hills of eastern Kentucky. Of course, my grandmother thought eleven was too young to marry, but thought it was smart to pick her out early and wait until she was old enough.

A few weeks later I had a conference with Elizabeth's mother. Her parents were divorced, and her father lived in York, Pennsylvania. Apparently I reminded Elizabeth of her father whom she missed. Instead of seeing me as a boyfriend, Elizabeth saw me as a father substitute. Way more appropriate, but a lot less flattering.

At Kenwood, most parents seemed satisfied if their child made it into the 'average' group. At Princsonia, parents wanted their child in the 'gifted' class. The school gave one IQ test only if the teacher requested it. If a student did not score 130 or higher, parents could have a private psychologist give the test. That was expensive, but those kids were more likely to pass. I strongly suspect it was more about the parents having bragging rights than what was best for their children.

Sadly, some of the students' parents were far from gifted.

Our school library had an unscheduled open system so a teacher could send students anytime during the day but only five at a time. I had five rows of student desks, so row one could go to the library on Mondays, row two on Tuesdays, and so on. The first five students would go and the others could go when they returned. One day I got an angry letter from a father accusing me a running an illegal 'library lottery' and he wanted it stopped immediately. I sent him a note explaining that it was the library's policy, not mine. Evidently that satisfied him, I never heard from him again.

I always enjoyed looking through the question box and came across one that I thought needed addressing.

"Someone referred to me as a weirdo in one of the notes in the question box. The writer didn't sign his or her name, which is OK, but I don't know who to thank. I know that being called a weirdo is an insult to some people, but I think it's a compliment. Weird just means different. Yes, you can be different in a bad way, but you can also be different in a good way. For example, being the smartest kid in the class makes you different, so it's weird. Being the best-looking kid in the class makes you different, so it's weird. It's OK to be different in my classroom. If you're not weird, it means you're just like everybody else. How boring is that? I don't want to be exactly like everyone else. I've always thought it was better to be one of the few than one of the many. I like the weird kids because they're more interesting. I'm pretty weird myself. If someone is weird in a bad way, don't be mean to them, don't make fun of them, just avoid them. Why waste your time on people you don't like? I think weird is a good thing. How many of you think you are weird?"

Virtually every hand in the room went up.

I began my first social studies class by showing the Earth to my students. I turned on the overhead projector, turned off the classroom lights, and held up the globe, demonstrating how it could be day on one side of the planet and night on the other. I spun it very slowly to illustrate sunrise and sunset. After turning the lights back on, I showed them the seven continents and tried to explain that it was warmer near the equator and colder at the poles. Teaching the difference between continents, countries, states, counties, and cities was a lot more complicated. I think it was a totally new concept for them.

Since there were five sixth grade classes and we were departmentalized, I had to teach the same lesson five times a day. I loved social studies so didn't really mind. It is also the reason my friends accuse me of repeating myself.

Elementary schools often have a lot of strange activities designed to keep the kids interested in school. This week we were celebrating Backwards Day, when all the kids were encouraged to wear their clothes backwards. To a few it meant wearing them inside out, but most wore the buttons and zippers in the back instead of the front. Other special days included Mismatched Sock Day, Tacky Day, Pajama Day, and Hat Day.

Although Princsonia was in a much more affluent neighborhood it was not without its problems.

Ryan Schuller caused a disruption nearly every day in my third period class. I called his mother to request a conference.

"Please have a seat," I said to Mrs. Schuller when she came in a few days later. "Ryan comes running into my classroom so fast that he has to put his foot against the wall to stop himself from crashing into it. Sometimes he just shouts out for no apparent reason. Ryan raises his books over his head and drops them to the floor just to make a loud noise. I talked to the other teachers and he acts the same way in their classes too. Ryan's not a bad kid and he isn't hurting anyone, but he does things just to get attention. Is he getting enough attention at home?"

"Who are you to question how I raise my son?" asked the immaculately dressed woman. "I take him to basketball practice after school, what more do you want? I know what he's like, I have to put up with him at home. At least you get paid for it!"

Several times that year I saw her picture in the newspaper for some activity with the Country Club or the Woman's Club. A few years later when Ryan was in high school, I heard he was arrested for selling drugs on campus.

Once the majority of students were able to write the names of all seven continents on a blank sheet of paper, I thought it was time to move to the next lesson.

"I want each one of you to pick any country in the world other than the United States. I'm going to pass a sign-up sheet around. Put your name on it and the country you select. Just remember to pick a country that's not already on the paper. I know I'm not Mrs. McGuinness, but today we're going to have a letter writing lesson. You're going to write a letter to the embassy of whatever country you select. Ask for information, maps, and pictures of their country, and use the school's address, written on the board, as your return address."

When they brought a postage stamp from home, I gave them envelopes and explained how to address them.

Internal politics was alive and well in the sixth grade at Princsonia Elementary. Each of us was in charge of our own curriculum, and Mrs. Tilton was the grade chairman in charge of sixth grade activities (parties, fieldtrips, etc.). Power had gone to her head. She taught reading and thought that was by far the most important subject. Mrs. Tilton was short, plump, and pompous, and always had a forced smile on her face, especially when she criticized someone, which was often. Her husband was a minister, so she felt that gave her exalted status in the community. She did not like all of my projects and told me to stick to reading the social studies textbook and having the students answer the questions at the end of each chapter. For reasons I never fully understood, she was less than fond of Mrs. McGuinness, the language arts (writing & spelling) teacher. Perhaps – only a guess – it was because Mrs. McGuinness was younger and better looking.

That hostility only made me like Mrs. McGuinness even more.

Last year we were encouraged to follow academic standards and benchmarks, this year they were required for reading and math. Science standards were set to begin next year, and social studies standards were still in development. They had trouble codifying and assessing patriotism and good judgement in voters. How do you decide which historical figures are important when the contributions of women and minorities have been diminished? There were those who wanted the role of white men taken out of textbooks completely because they had dominated too long.

While we waited for replies from the embassies, I taught about Ancient Sumer, and Ancient Egypt. Sumer was the earliest civilization in Mesopotamia and gave us the Code of Hammurabi, and Egypt is known for pyramids, pharaohs, and the invention of papyrus.

The students acted as if they had never gotten mail before when their replies from the embassies started arriving. Their faces were full of smiles and they were eager to show off the pictures, maps, and brochures they received, and were jealous if other students received more than they did. Russia usually sent the most material. Some students decided to write to more embassies.

I gave the students an outline to follow and assigned them to write a five to ten- page report on the country they selected.

My education classes taught that students remember a low percentage of what they read and a lower percentage of what they hear, but a high percentage of what they teach. For that reason, I had each student present their report to the entire class.

First and last names on papers became even more of an obsession with me because, having five classes a day, I sometimes had five Johns, six Marys, and four Anns. In my whole teaching career I never came across a student named Brenford. I was named after my grandfather and have no idea what his parents were thinking. My grandmother's name was Ethel; I have never had a student named that either.

I went to an office supply store and had a custom set of rubber stamps made that said, 'EXCELLENT,' 'VERY GOOD,' 'MESSY,' 'LATE,' 'DO OVER,' and most importantly, 'PUT YOUR FIRST AND LAST NAME ON YOUR PAPER.' The other teachers gave me the nickname 'the Mad Stamper.'

From time to time we experienced a sudden blast of foul air of a biological nature coming from the back of the room. The students giggled and pointed to each other. The hotter the outside temperature, the worse the smell. Some of them were pretty rank. A truly hot day could curl your hair and cause your eyes to water. As the weather cooled, the blasts became less frequent and gradually faded away.

Being departmentalized meant we only had one subject to make lesson plans for instead of five. The bad news is that if we had parent conferences about academics all five of us had to attend so it meant five times more meetings.

Teaching gives you an insight into how other people live and it is really an eye opener. In one parent conference, I learned that one mother allowed her eleven-year-old daughter to live with a twenty-year-old man down the street who needed someone to cook and clean for him. She claimed she kept an eye on her daughter because she frequently saw her walking to and from the school bus stop. Coming from a more affluent home does not necessarily mean coming from a better one. Another mother claimed she stopped her boyfriend from having sex with her daughter and, instead of throwing him out, she put her daughter on birth control pills.

One parent made an appointment with me to discuss a personal matter.

"How can I help you Mrs. Swanson?

"This is probably for all of Judy's teacher, but I'm too embarrassed to discuss it with them," said the mother. "About two weeks ago Judy and I were walking downtown and I noticed a used condom on the sidewalk. I couldn't decide whether or not to mention it hoping she wouldn't step on it, or to point it out and risk her asking what it was. She needs to know about all that but I'm just too embarrassed to tell her. Can you do it?"

"Unfortunately, this is my first year at Princsonia so I don't know what the policy is on sex education, but I'll ask around and find out for you."

I mentioned it to both the school nurse and principal. The nurse knew someone who made presentations to schools and had separate movies for the girls and the boys. The principal approved and a date was set. Permission notes were sent home for the parents to sign. The girls would go to the cafeteria and the boys to the library. Since I was the only male teacher in the sixth grade, I showed an instructional film showing the boys what would happen to their bodies during puberty and had to stand in front of approximately seventy-five boys to talk to them about penises, scrotums, and hair growth in new places. It was one of the longest hours in my life and I am sure most of what I said was drowned out by their embarrassed giggles. The girls were given free tampon samples and told not to mention them to the boys. The boys were unhappy that they didn't get a bag of goodies too, and were even more annoyed when the girls wouldn't tell them what they had gotten.

Sadly, one hour is not enough time to adequately cover the topic, but administrators were afraid to allow any more time. Perhaps sex education should be dealt with at home, but most parents were too embarrassed. The guest speaker was angry because dozens of high school girls got pregnant without knowing that free birth control was available. No school official was allowed to tell them about it.

The next morning Shawna Beauchamp walked into my classroom dressed like a gypsy with a scarf over her hair, large dangly earrings, a large tacky necklace, and a long skirt. When I asked her what was going on, she replied by pulling a volleyball covered in aluminum foil out of a shopping bag and said it was her crystal ball. Mrs. McGuinness had assigned them to write a book review and today they were giving their oral presentations.

Shawna put her 'crystal ball' on my desk and began telling my fortune. Just then the principal walked in with a camera. Mr. Adams was taking pictures around the school for a PTA presentation and just happened to walk into my room at that moment. He claimed he had no idea what was going on.

Shawna was brilliantly creative, but the other students regarded her as a nerd. Instead of collecting Teddy Bears, Shawna collected stuffed hyenas, which are hard to find. She thought laughing hyenas were misunderstood. Jenell, one of the teachers' aides, told me that was because Shawna felt misunderstood herself.

With a smile on her face, Mrs. Tilton tore into Mrs. McGuinness for overstepping her boundaries. Mrs. Tilton said she was in charge of reading, so Mrs. McGuinness had no business assigning book reports.

"Written book reports do fall under language arts, and oral presentations are 'speeches' and they also fall under language arts," explained Mrs. McGuinness.

"We'll just see what the principal has to say about this,"

said Mrs. Tilton storming away.

I was thrilled because it took the spotlight off me and my social studies projects.

The Ancient Greeks wore a simple garment called a chiton, made from a single piece of cloth, about the size of a tablecloth, folded, pinned at the shoulders, and tied around the waist with a cord or ribbon. I had my grandparents make me two of them, one in my size and one to fit my students.

I introduced the Ancient Greek unit by letting one student in each class wear the smaller chiton. That grabbed their attention. I talked about the different periods of Ancient Greek History: Minoan, Mycenean, Hellenic; the Golden Age, and the Hellenistic period. I mostly focused on their way of life, how they dressed, what they ate, their educational system, traditions, art, architecture, and what they did for fun.

One day I dressed in a chiton and told Greek myths all period. I knew I was doing a great job when I was acting out 'Damon and Pythias.' I got to the point in the story where Damon was tied to a post awaiting execution and saw Pythias in the distance running toward them, two or three students turned to see what I was pretending to look at.

It was impossible not to notice the ancient Greeks' casual attitude toward nudity. In fact, the original meaning of the word 'gymnasium' meant a place to exercise naked.

One day two boys came up to me with an art book and pointed to the crotch of a statue of a boy about their age.

"Mr. Williams, look!"

"Back in ancient times, people didn't think the human body was dirty," I replied.

"I know but look, he has fur!"

"That happens to boy's bodies as they turn into men. Hair also starts growing in their armpits and on their face. Remember, we talked about that one day."

I hoped their parents knew it was time to have 'the talk' with them.

My unit ended with Greek Day. All of the students were asked to wear chitons to school. One boy wore a chiton made from a red and white checkered tablecloth. The cafeteria made a Greek meal, fish, cheese, olives, and vegetables that could be eaten with the fingers. The whole sixth grade went outside so students could recreate most of the events from the ancient pentathlon: foot races, broad jump with weights, Greek wrestling in olive oil, and throwing a Frisbee. The principal would not allow us to throw javelins or a discus. Even the P.E. teacher dressed up in a chiton.

Other students pointed and laughed at my students, so I explained that the Ancient Greeks were very proud and looked down on all non-Greeks. In fact, the word 'barbarian' originally meant anyone who could not speak Greek.

At the end of the day more than one student came up to me to say they would remember that day for as long as they lived.

Mrs. Tilton was not happy with it, "You spent five weeks covering Ancient Greece. Last year the social studies teacher covered it in only two and didn't make a big fuss about it. Make wiser use of your time. Think about the topics you won't be able to cover because you spent so much time on this."

Her criticism fell on deaf ears because Mr. Adams was happy when the Greek Day pictures appeared in the local newspaper. Principals love good publicity.

In cooperation with my lesson, Mrs. McGuinness gave the students a creative writing assignment about what it would be like to live in Ancient Greece.

WOULD I LIKE TO LIVE IN ATHENS?

By Chris Chin

I would have liked waiting for the future. I might have been one of the great people of Athens. Either a general or a king. I couldn't have been a king long though, because of democracy.

I would have followed my teacher long ago, Socrates or Plato.

I would also want to live back then because I wouldn't mind going around bare. I'll tell you something, it would be comfortable.

The houses were neat, you could get a sunburn without going outside.

I would like to enter the Olympics and win to show off in front of my friends.

By the way, I would probably know a lot of people, for instance, Mr. Williams, a real good friend of mine.

I would like the idea of starting my own business, like building furniture, making pottery, or selling olive oil.

I'll tell you something, I'd rather live in Athens than Sparta.

Again I took students grocery shopping for the Christmas party. The price of cologne rose so I received fewer bottles this year, but 'oooed' and 'awwwed' over eight more mugs. Instead of everyone buying individual gifts, some parents got together and gave a nicer gift. One group of parents presented me with a nice punch bowl.

What I saw at Princsonia was also a culture shock, but in a different way. A few of the parents were hosting co-ed sleepovers. No one asked my opinion, but I am not comfortable with eleven and twelve-year-old boys seeing girls - who are not family members - in their pajamas. Thoughts are already in their heads, why increase the temptation to go exploring after the lights go out. OK, maybe that makes me a prude. Pajamas are perfect clothing to wear in your OWN space, but NOT outside the home. I know our school had Pajama Day, but I never participated in that. I do not wear pajamas anyway so would be arrested if I did participate. At the risk of sounding like a hypocrite, I have no objection to families going to nude beaches because that is in a very public space. I am suspicious of any child who is not curious. Sleepovers are much more intimate, and the lights go out. I am not as concerned about what they see as with what they do. It is a sick society whose values allow children to watch hundreds of murders on TV while simultaneously teaching that their own bodies are obscene.

Perhaps my concerns came from frequently finding notes like these:

Dear Honey,

I know you probably don't like me, but I love you. Please don't hate me.

Love,

Joan

George,

     I really do love you and don't want to break up, but I will if you want to and if you love me. If you love me how do you do this to me? It really hurts to find out that you play around with other girls.

     Love you,

     Gertrude

Fred,

     Did you really want to French kiss, neck, and feel-out?

     Yes or no

     Circle one

     I love you,

     Alice

Dear Herman,

I don't care if you don't whont to go with me, but I steal love you even if you steal go with someone else. You are the sweetyest boy I have ever seen and the most handsomest boy in the hole wolrd.

Love you always,

Amanda

Signs started appearing on restroom doors and in the hallways saying, 'WILLIAMS' WINGS.' New signs went up every day for a week. I had no idea what was going on and neither did most of the kids. Then the signs said, 'Wing Fashion show in Mr. Williams class TOMORROW.'

The next day Shawna Beauchamp and another girl asked if they could talk to the class about something. One girl read the description while five girls strutted around the room wearing wings made from poster board. The wings came in different colors and some were covered in glitter or aluminum foil. There were plaid wings, polka-dot wings, and even designer wings with pictures on them.

I asked her what was this all about and she said I had taught a lesson on advertising and propaganda and that gave her the idea. As I said, Shawna was brilliant, and I loved her creativity. Needless to say she was one of my favorites.

Spring Break finally arrived. My three favorite vacation places in the world were Manhattan, Sarasota, and Key West. I went to Key West over spring break. It is a great place to relax because there is little to do there besides eat, drink, shop, and fish, and I don't fish. Nearly every bar has live entertainment. I knew Hat Day was coming up soon on the school calendar, so I bought a special hat for the occasion.

I came back to school to find a note on my desk.

Dear Mr. Williams,

I had fun last week, except my favorite teacher wasn't there. I expect to see you when we get back to school, in fact, I'll even look forward to it. Did you know that you're just like my dad? He teases me too!

Hat Day was different from other silly dress-up days because it was also a fund raiser. Students were not allowed to wear hats indoors except on Hat Day, and only if they donated one dollar. A rubber stamp was placed on the back of their hand giving permission to wear a hat for the day. In Key West, I bought an over-sized magician's hat with a stuffed bunny on the brim. The rabbit was attached with Velcro. I quickly got tired of kids jumping up to grab the bunny,

I wanted to talk to one of the other teachers about something and noticed a jar of individually wrapped hard candy on the fourth grade teacher's desk.

"What's that all about," I asked.

"Sometimes you ask your class a question and no one wants to answer. All I have to do is reach into the jar and hands go up all over the room. You ought to try it, it's a great attention getter. It also helps with behavior if I give one to the most improved. Just don't give them out too frequently or they'll come to expect them."

Instead of putting candy in a jar on my desk, I carried several in my pocket. Some of the kids started calling me the 'Candy Man.'

Because I went to the Florida Education Association convention last year, I was selected to be Princsonia's representative at the school board level chapter. They were starting a new political action committee and I was one of about twenty-five teachers who showed up for the convening meeting. The first item of business was to elect officers. An acquaintance I barely knew nominated me for president.

Each candidate was asked to give a brief campaign speech.

"I wouldn't even vote for myself," I told them. "I have a general idea how politics is supposed to work, but I'm only here so I can learn how it actually works in the real world. I respectfully decline"

I was elected vice-president and the guy who nominated me was elected president. About three weeks later he resigned, and I became the new president. I did not see that coming.

Florida was divided into districts. I attended a meeting of the eight or ten presidents of the local political action committees in our district. Our names were put into a bowl and mine was drawn out as the representative for our district. I suddenly wound up in one of the top positions at the state level of the Florida Education Association's Political Action Committee. I will not pretend, even for a minute, that I belonged there, but I was one of the eight people on the committee that interviewed all the candidates running for statewide offices. It meant flying up to Tallahassee on the weekends. After interviewing the gubernatorial candidates, I nominated that we endorse Bob Graham. He later said he would have dropped out of the race if we had not endorsed him. He not only won, twice, but went on to win three terms in the US Senate.

I have lived in Florida since I was seven years old but was born in Kentucky. My mother wrote to the governor of Kentucky and told him about my work on the political action committee, and he awarded me the title of 'Kentucky Colonel.'

As the weather warmed up, the blasts of foul air began

again. I could tell by the expressions of the kids in the back of the room when I only had about thirty seconds before being enveloped in an invisible cloud of smelly noxious gases. We eventually figured it was coming from the air-conditioner, which hung from the ceiling, instead of one of the students with a digestive issue. A maintenance request was sent in to the county office. It took about three weeks for a maintenance man to come to our classroom. For the record, it is impossible to hold a class's attention when a workman is banging on equipment in the back of the room. He did not find any problem there, so went up on the roof. The plumbing air vent from the classroom bathroom was too close to the intake of the air-conditioner. There had been a stack pipe that lifted the foul air above the air-conditioner intake, but it was missing. He replaced it and the foul odors stopped.

As I was walking to my car in the parking lot at the end of the school day, Mr. Adams, the principal, stopped me and said he wanted to talk to me about something important. He did not have time then but wanted to see me in his office tomorrow.

I drove home wondering what I had done wrong. I did

not sleep well that night fearing I was about to be fired.

The principal was absent the next day, so I had another day and night to worry.

When I finally made it to the principal's office, he was merely concerned about the conflict between Mrs. Tilton and Mrs. McGuinness. It had nothing to do with me. I was so relieved that I did not catch anything he said except that he wanted me to act as peacemaker.

Greatly relieved I returned to my classroom to find a note from Mrs. Tilton on my desk. It said someone from the local Rotary Club would visit every sixth grade classroom that day to tell the students about an annual speech writing competition. Students make a three to five-minute speech on one point from their Four Way Test.

FOUR WAY TEST

1. Is it the TRUTH?

2. Is it FAIR to all concerned?

3. Will it build GOODWILL and BETTER FRIENDSHIPS?

4. Will it be BENEFICIAL to all concerned?

The Four Way Test is brilliant and should hang on the wall of every classroom and every politician's office in the country.

The speeches would be written in language arts, but all five sixth grade teachers would be the judges of the oral presentations. We were given itemized score sheets listing criteria we were supposed to judge and how many points were in each category. It took three days to listen to and evaluate all the speeches. After tallying the scores, the clear winner was Shawna Beauchamp.

Substitutes were hired and Mrs. McGuinness and I accompanied Shawna to the Rotary luncheon where she gave her speech to the local chapter.

As president of the FEA's local Political Action Committee, I was reminded that even though we had endorsed a few candidates, I could not wear any campaign badges or even put bumper stickers on my car unless I parked off-campus. I understood that, and the school handbook stated students were not to wear badges, t-shirts, or insignias from out of school organizations in order to avoid conflict.

One day I noticed one of my students wearing a campaign badge and asked him to remove it. He did and I thought that was the end of it until I was called into the principal's office the next day.

"I got a very angry phone call from the Pattersons last night," began Mr. Adams. "Jeff didn't mind when you ask him to remove the campaign button he was wearing, but his parents did. They were furious and said you were stifling his right of free expression."

"But the school's handbook says that students and staff aren't allowed to wear campaign buttons, logos of outside organizations, or gang insignias."

"The handbook was made right here at school and won't stand up in court."

"You mean I got in trouble for enforcing the rules."

"They're not exactly rules, more like ideal suggestions. If a student wants to wear a campaign badge, we have to let them. If the parents decide to sue, I can't support you, but I don't think that will happen. I calmed them down and told them Jeff could wear the badge today."

I was so angry I went back to my classroom and threw my copy of the handbook into the trash can. In Florida, teachers were on Annual Contract for the first three years and might not be hired back for any reason the principal chooses. The decision to put me on Continuing Contract was coming up soon so I knew I needed to keep my mouth shut.

Jeff wore the badge that day and I pretended not to notice.

Just a day or two later, Eduardo Hernandez come into my class wearing a hat. Wearing a hat indoors was one of Mr. Adams' pet peeves and I needed to stay in his good graces, so I asked Eduardo to remove it. He did, but it was back on his head about fifteen minutes later. Again I asked him to take it off, and again he did. Ten minutes later he was wearing the hat again.

I took Eduardo's hat and told him to write a letter to his mother telling her what happened.

*Mom, I was wearing my hat in Mr. Williams' room and he told
me to take it off and I did, then I put it back on, then he told me
to take it off again and I didn't and he took it from me and won't
give it back unless you sign this paper.*

The note came back signed, I gave him the hat and never
saw it again.

Mrs. Tilton was still clashing with Mrs. McGuinness. It
was almost a game, Mrs. McGuinness and I sometimes tried to
guess what Mrs. Tilton would complain about that day.

Toward the end of the school year, Mrs. McGuinness
came into my room in an unusually good mood. Mrs. Tilton had
not said a word to her all day. We joked Mrs. Tilton must not be
feeling well.

Rumors were frequent, and while most of them were not
true, enough of them were so they could not be dismissed. We
heard one rumor that the principal was not coming back next
year, and another that Mrs. Tilton was not coming back. We
were not sure whether either was true, but they were both
possibilities.

The next morning Mrs. McGuinness met me in the hallway saying she had just heard a new rumor that Mr. Adams would be replaced by Mr. Thomas Chapman from Southside Elementary."

"I heard he was terrible."

"I heard that too."

"Oh great, we get rid of Tilton and get Chapman!"

I had no idea that Mrs. Tilton was standing right behind me. While it was true that I was not overly fond of her but wouldn't have said something to deliberately hurt her feelings.

She pretended not to hear and walked away leaving me feeling guilty the rest of the day.

As I was leaving for the day, I stopped in the office to check my mailbox. There was my letter granting me Continuing Contract. It was all I could do not to shout for joy.

I took my parents and grandparents out to a nice restaurant to celebrate and was a little surprised when the next day my students knew where we went and even what I had ordered.

The principal called the faculty into the library for our

last meeting of the school year. He wanted us to review the school handbook before sending it to the printer for the next school year.

I raised my hand and said, "I ask that the rules in the handbook either be enforced or completely done away with."

That put him on the defensive. Mr. Adams became evasive and tried to ignore my comments.

That upset me even more. I felt anger pushing reason aside. I do not remember exactly what I said but loud angry words poured out of me. That was very unusual for me since I am usually calm and quiet.

Other teachers, most of whom agreed with me, told me later that my face was red and the veins in my neck stood out. At least I got it out of my system.

One teacher walked up to me after the meeting and said, "My my, now that you have Continuing Contract, you're opening your mouth, aren't you?"

That evening while reading the newspaper, I looked at my horoscope, something I rarely did.

Do not force issues. Be careful, kind, and diplomatic.

Steer clear of confrontations.

SIX

CREATIVE WRTING ASSIGNMENTS

MR. SNAIL GOES TO SCHOOL

One day Mr. Snail decided he would go to school. He started at the beginning of Spring Vacation and made it there just as the kids were coming back.

First he went to the office.

"Hummm, very interesting," said Mr. Snail.

People were talking, phones were ringing, and papers were being shuffled. After he watched the people and things in the office, he decided to go outside.

People were just going out to Phys. Ed. Mr. Snail watched them get ready to play.

"Hummm, very interesting," said Mr. Snail.

The game first started as a girl hit a little round thing with a long object and would run around in a circle, stepping on square things on the ground. When she would get back to where she started, half of the girls would yell, "Yea, another point!" Of course Mr. Snail didn't know what this meant.

After Mr. Snail got tired of watching the young humans, he decided to go inside and up the stairs. He started crawling. The first door he came to said Mrs. Sirota, 6th Grade. He crawled in. Everyone was looking in books and writing, while the teacher, Mrs. Sirota, was helping a student.

After he watched this a little while, he decided to go across the hall. The door said, Mr. Montgomery, 6th Grade.

He crawled under the door and saw the kids jumping up and down on the desks and throwing paper airplanes, while the teacher, Mr. Montgomery, slept and slept.

"Hummm, very interesting," said Mr. Snail.

Mr. Snail decided to go across the auditorium. He was in luck, this door said Mrs. Allred, 5th Grade.

"This room should be very interesting," said Mr. Snail.

He crawled under the door and saw a few people whispering and breaking the silence, while the teacher was writing on the chalkboard.

Mr. Snail decided he would go across the hall and see what was over there. He crawled slowly out of the room and across the hall. This door said Mr. Williams, 5th Grade.

"Hummm, very interesting," said Mr. Snail.

He crawled under the door and this would be his last trip to this school, because what else did he see but the kids running around the room with paper hats on and the teacher, Mr. Williams, was jumping up and down on his desk yelling, "Live it up!" Mr. Williams almost stepped on Mr. Snail as he was ripping off his clothes to go outside and "streak."

Mr. Snail was so disgusted that he left the room, went down stairs, and out of the building.

Oh, if you are wondering about Mr. Williams, he is spending his time at the funny farm sunbathing, with is bathing suit on, of course!

ONE DAY AT SEA

The story starts when we were on our voyage to Greece, which we have been studying for the past twelve weeks, which seems more like twelve years. We all knew either we were going to get sea sick or Greece sick, which ever came first. I think at the moment the majority of the crowd was sea sick. We were all hanging over the side, let's just say we were turning green.

Hours later we were all hungry and it was Mr. Williams' turn to cook, it was awful. When he was gone we hid the junk in number 4 lifeboat.

All of a sudden water started gushing into the ship from a hole in the hull. Mr. Williams jumped under, thinking it was a *shower. I pulled him out and we jumped into number 4 lifeboat. There were six other people in the boat.*

Mr. Williams grabbed the wheel, that's why we got lost from the other lifeboats. With our luck, you would know a half an hour later we ran out of gas.

I thought and I thought, I had an idea. I remembered the food we had put in the boat. It came in useful. If it gave the motor as much gas as it gave us, our problems would be solved. It worked, in fifteen minutes we had traveled a hundred miles. Boy, was that stuff strong!

I saw land, but we could not stop. The boat blew up with all our supplies.

Mr. Williams was found kissing the sand. I knew he was happy, but that happy?

It was about noon, I pulled Mr. Williams up from the sand, but all of a sudden he started kissing me! I gave him a good slap or two and he snapped out of it. We were on a deserted island.

I said we have to find a cave or some place to stay. Mr. Williams said something about looking for a hotel. I just rolled my eyes.

We split up into three groups, I got stuck with guess who. We went straight into the woods. You've heard of laughing hyenas, as soon as that hyena saw Mr. Williams, he laughed and laughed so hard, we were miles away before the sound died down.

I saw a cave and told Mr. Williams to stay there while I got the others. I told him to fix dinner while I was gone. I knew that was one of the worst ideas I could have thought of.

On the way back to the cave I saw him wondering through the woods. I asked what was he doing out here. He said he was looking for the Tourist Information Center. I angrily told him there weren't any information stations, this is an island, not Disney World.

Mr. Williams said OK, he would look for a telephone booth then. When I asked about dinner, Mr. Williams said he would also keep an eye out for a restaurant.

The next day Mr. Williams got lost looking for a mailbox.
We searched and searched for him. When we found him, he
showed us his new girlfriend. She weighed 350 pounds, looked
like she was 70, and had a face like a bullfrog. Mr. Williams
didn't know she was the chief's daughter, he always had a taste
for royalty.

The chief thought we had captured her and sent 150
native warriors after us. While they were after us, Mr. Williams
had an itch. He lifted his pant leg to scratch it, all 150 natives
fell laughing and laughing and laughing. They laughed so hard
and oud that a nearby ship heard them and we were saved.

A DAY IN SPARTA

6:00 – I wake up glad it's Sunday and sleep for ten
more minutes.

6:30 – I am first in the line for breakfast. We're
having mush, yum yum.

7:15 – Morning exercise, I accidentally speared the sergeant, may he rest in peace!

8:00 – I got E. Pluribuscharlie Atlasium's autograph.

9:00 – We practice clubbing, I only got three stiches.

10:00 – For two hours we "streak."

12:00 – Lunch, Helen of Troy walks in and I fall over backwards into my mush.

1:00 – Free Time.

2:30 – Exercise till 5:00.

5:00 – Target practice, today is my lucky day, I got three rabbits, a bear, and my instructor.

8:00 – Sundown, time for bed.

10:00 – We raid the local farmer since we didn't have dinner.

A VISIT TO ATHENS

Once I was walking down the street and all of the sudden swoosh! I was falling in space and when I hit the ground, I found I was in Ancient Greece. I saw the Parthenon and the Acropolis. There were some clothes, Greek clothes, so I put them on. I went over several hills till I go downtown. As I was looking around, a man came up to me and asked why I wasn't in school. I ran away from him. As I was running I saw some kids. They came up to me and asked me to go with them. I went to their school and I saw there were no girls! Then I remembered what Mr. Williams said. He told us only boys went to school, the girls stayed home with their mothers. After school I was walking down the street and a huge man came up to me and said, "Hi, son, let's go home." He thought I was his son. I went along with him as it was dinner time. After dinner we went to the gymnasium, where the Greeks take off their clothes and rub olive oil over their bodies. Oops, aaaaa!

Ugh! Here I am back in my own bed. Wait till I tell Mr. Williams and Mom! Will they ever be surprised!

A DAY IN ROME

I woke up this morning ready and roarin' to do a day's work. I pulled on my toga, hopped into my chariot, hopped out of my chariot, put the horses on my chariot, hopped in my chariot, hopped out of my chariot, got my lunch, and forgetting my chariot, I ran all the way to work.

I work at a bath house. Everything went smoothly all morning. During lunch break I ordered the strongest rum in the house. I took out my sausage and cheese and I went to visit my friend, who works under the hot pool. He was having trouble with the fire.

I said, "As long as the fire is so low, why not put it out and build a new one?"

He said, "OK," and I threw the rum on it to put it out.

Surprise! The fire flared up and I heard several yells from above. I leaped up the stairs and met steam and a lot of mad, red-faced Romans.

I dropped my cheese so I could run better and it landed in the steam room. An awful smell of limburger rose in the air. That took everyone's breath away.

I ran all the way home only to be run over by my own chariot, which was still in my front yard.

As I went into the house, my wife asked me what happened at work today?

I said, "Nothing, it was just an ordinary day!"

LOST ON AN ISLAND

As I recollect, Kevin, John, Andy, Tina, Mr. Williams, and I were going on a tour of a so-called deserted island somewhere in the South Pacific.

We were sailing there on Mr. Williams' yacht named, S.S. Mephistophecles. We were about forty miles from the nearest piece of land. I was steering the yacht and Mr. Williams and the rest of the crew were asleep on the lower deck in lounge chairs. Mr. Williams' obnoxious snoring threw the yacht into a violent thirty degree turn.

Suddenly Mr. Williams got up and came over to me and yelled, "Derek, whatda' turn the ship like that for?!!!"

To which I replied, "Sir, I did not turn the yacht."

"Well then, who in the name of Eric von Strugglebergershagnasty III did?" screamed Mr. Williams.

"Your snoring, Sir," said I, in a very calm way compared to Mr. Williams' raging voice.

"Huh," sputtered Mr. Williams, "that's preposterous....I NEVER snore, hmph!"

To which John replied waking from the quarrel, "How would you know if you were asleep when you did it?"

Greatly reddened and embarrassed, Mr. Williams said, "I oughta know when I snore and when I don't."

"True, Sir, you ought to know, but you don't," said I as I stared awkwardly into the ocean.

John noticed this and said, "Say, Derek, why are you looking out there so hard, there's nothin' out there but a whole bunch of ....," John suddenly stopped and saw the same unbelievable sight I saw.

"Mr. Williams, look!" exclaimed John.

Mr. Williams also was astonished at the sight which we all wanted to see for at least ten hours.

"Hand lo- uh- I mean uh – stand ho – uh- well – uh- ho land – uh- er- buh ---," stuttered Mr. Williams.

"Here Sir, let me help you," said I. "Ahem (clearing my throat, of course) Land ho," I stated in a very clam manner.

Almost the very second I said those very simple words, which Mr. Williams couldn't seem to get out, the entire crew suddenly arose and flew to the upper deck.

"Did someone say land ho?" queried Tina.

"Indeed, someone did," said I.

"I didn't hear it," said Kevin.

To which Mr. Williams said, "Shame be upon you."

While everyone was trying to get over that, the ship crashed into a large boulder on an even larger island. All of us violently hit the deck (not by order, of course). After we all recovered I noticed murky water gushing in from a four foot hole in the hull of the ship.

I realized the only way to get off the boat was to let down a rope or jump off the side. I chose to jump. I climbed up on the rail and slipped. I did a perfect belly-buster. The rest of them used the rope.

We swam to shore and I decided to explore the island. I wandered into a dense growth of palm trees and bushes. I stumbled over a few and landed in front of a cave. I went in.

It was very very very dark and damp. I groped around and felt my eyes grow wider and wider. I ran into something very hairy. At first I thought Mr. Williams had grown his beard again, but I realized that he did not come into the cave with me. Quickly, I ran out and got Andy. I told him about the 'thing' in the cave. That made him want to explore a different part of the island, but I dragged him anyway.

This time he ran into it and it fell on him. I grabbed it and found out that it was very light. Outside I could see that it was only a large palm leaf.

The ship was useless, so we had to stay on the island. All our food was gone and hunger sat it.

Finally Andy said, "Dereck, why don't you climb one of these trees and get some coconuts for us?"

"Because I don't want to—You'll never get me up that tree!"

Of course in five minutes I found myself at the top of thirty-five-foot tree, throwing coconuts down. I saw something I thought we would never see again, a ship.

Without fear I jumped and landed on my feet. They hurt so much I couldn't walk for the next five minutes.

By the time I got down to the beach, the others had already jumped aboard and were sailing away without me.

"Who needs 'em?" said I, in a very calm voice.

SEVEN

The rumor about Mrs. Tilton not coming back to Princsonia was true, but the other rumor about Mr. Adams being replaced by Mr. Chapman was not. Instead our new principal would be Mrs. Virginia Harris, who previously taught typing and bookkeeping at the local high school. Since this would be her first year as principal, none of us had a clue what to expect. High school typing was the most useful class I had ever taken so I had high hopes for her.

If a long boring faculty meeting on the first day of pre-planning week was any indication, then Mrs. Harris was well on her way toward filling the shoes of a principal.

Besides meetings, planning our lessons, and decorating our classrooms, one of our important jobs is to review our homeroom's permanent record folders. Permanent records begin in kindergarten and follow students up to high school. I have no idea what happens to them after that. We go through them to look at photographs, past report card grades, achievement test scores, and health concerns. I try not to read past teachers' comments until I have already formed an opinion about a student.

Such comments are meant to let the next teacher know what to expect, but I prefer giving the students the benefit of the doubt because sometimes those comments do not hold up. A perfect example is a new student we received last year about two/thirds of the way through the year. We were warned that he had already been kicked out of his last two schools for attacking his teachers. One time it was a physical attack; the other time he threw a lit firecracker under the teacher's chair. When Terry arrived, he was an angry, rough looking kid - bigger than me. As if his size wasn't intimidating enough, he had fresh sores on his knuckles that looked as if he had been ramming his fists into a concrete block wall. To be honest, he scared me, so I gave him some space. Bravery does not mean having no fear, it means not letting your fear stop you.

It soon became apparent that he was a gentle giant. His knuckles healed and instead of being a ruffian, it was obvious that he had a very effeminate disposition which was quite incongruous with his tough appearance and size. I could easily imagine his anger stemmed from being ridiculed for that. I discovered Terry was a wonderful kid, kind, cooperative, and helpful, but below average academically. I assumed his past problems were due to prejudice, either racial, homophobia, or both. He loved music so I brought in my Celine Dion, Cher, and Johnny Mathis CDs and printed out the lyrics for him to read while he listened. The other students liked him and he fit right in at Princsonia. He was making progress by the end of the year and I wished I had more time to work with him. The saddest thing about teaching is getting attached to students and never hearing about them again.

Among my new group of students, Kasey Storti, whose family had just moved to Florida from Rhode Island, claimed to have a stomachache on the first day of the school year and asked to go to the clinic. She looked pale so I did not hesitate. When it happened every day that week, the nurse thought it might be a psychosomatic fear of school. She explained her feelings to the parents, adding that she was not a psychologist so was not actually qualified to diagnose. The nurse suggested that Kasey stay in the classroom to see if the symptoms went away. It was a little unnerving to have a student in the room who might throw up like a geyser at any moment, but it worked. Once Kasey learned that she was not going home, her stomachaches went away. She had been afraid of going to a new school where she did not know anyone. Once she made a few friends, she began to enjoy it.

August is Florida's hottest month, but Septembers are close. The air-conditioner in our classroom broke down and it reached well over ninety degrees inside. While the air-conditioner was no longer delivering bad smells, the kids certainly were. The homework assignment that night was to take a bath or shower, with soap.

Math flash cards were fairly common, but I came across a

set of geography flash cards with the shape of countries on them. I used them to play a game of streetcar. Two students stood side-by-side and were shown a flash card. The first to identify it moved on to the next desk. The first student in the class who makes it back to his or her starting point won.

Most of my students came from good homes, but not all of them. One of my girls had a crick in her neck. When I asked her why, she said it was not her turn to sleep in the bed that night.

Some of these kids were so desperate for attention that they would make up stories just to have someone notice them. I never knew whether to believe their stories or not. One boy made up a story about his father taking him skydiving. That never happened. He just wanted other kids to think his father spent time with him.

One girl told me her parents had divorced and married other people. She told me her mother was leaving her second husband and going back to her first husband who was also leaving his second wife. I had no idea any of it was a secret until her stepfather came to school the next week looking for her. His wife had cleared out their joint bank account and disappeared with her clothes, her car, her children, and their furniture. Mrs. Hazen, the math teacher, told a similar story that happened in her class. One of her students told her that she, her brother, and sister were leaving their father and going to live with their mother. She even called the home and spoke to the other sister who told her it was all a lie. A week later, they had indeed run away.

I walked into my new condo just in time to hear the phone ring.

"Hello?"

"Hi, how do you like living on your own?" asked my cousin, Ellen, from Ohio.

"So far I love it. I miss mother's cooking but don't have to hear her getting on me about leaving my shoes in the living room."

"What I'm calling about is that I want to join DAR, Daughters of the American Revolution, so I can get my kids in CAR."

"CAR?"

"Children of the American Revolution. I need birth and death certificates and family Bible genealogy records for all our family going back to the Revolutionary War. I need help getting started. Do you know mamau and papau's exact birthdays?"

I gave her the dates and we chatted a while longer before ending the call.

Our grandfather said we descended from Daniel Boone's sister, Mary, and the majority of our ancestors came from the British Isles. Maybe that explains our British reserve or reluctance to show emotion. We're not a family of huggers.

Maybe that's why I never got used students hugging me, grabbing me, leaning against me, or touching me. I never knew if it was because they hungered for human contact or if they felt it would get them more attention.

One day a boy gave me a hug with his face against my chest and said, "You smell."

He never said whether I smelled good or bad. I wore cologne but the stuff my students gave me at Christmas was the cheap drug store variety. I switched to more expensive colognes. The difference between good cologne and bad cologne is not how good it smells, but how long the scent lasts. It's common for most men splash a few drops on their hands and rub it onto their face and neck. I read an article that recommended putting it on your chest and allowing your body heat to waft the scent up around your face. Instead of three or four spritzes, I use twice that. Now you know why my scent enters a room before I do.

Teachers notice the brightest students, the weakest students, and the behavior problems, but sometimes the kids in the middle do not get as much attention as they need. Nick Calvert was a pretty ordinary student, average grades, average looks, and average behavior. Because of that, I selected him to wear the chiton in class when we got to our Ancient Greek unit. I just happened to have my camera at school that day and took a picture of him wearing it. His mother loved the picture and invited me to their home to take a family picture to use as their Christmas card.

The day after the photo session, Nick had a noticeable twinkle in his eye and uncharacteristically raised his hand to answer questions. The other teachers noticed it too and overnight his grades went from C's to A's. Shirley Tucker, his homeroom teacher sent him to the guidance counselor to find out what was going on.

Up until then he felt unnoticed at school so why should he bother to try? The teacher - me - going to his house made him feel important. Teachers did not go to everyone's house, but I went to his. His achievement test scores showed slightly over a three-year improvement that year, all because he felt noticed.

A few years later I was invited to his home for Nick's high school graduation party.

The day after I wore my chiton and told Greek myths, I felt the worst pain of my life as I was driving to school. It felt like someone rammed an ice pick into my back at the belt level. I turned the car around and barely made it back into the house before collapsing to the floor. I grabbed the phone and called the school telling them to get a substitute for me. I then called my doctor's office to beg for an appointment. The nurse I spoke to told me to go straight to the emergency room, not the doctor's office. It was the only time in my life that I wanted them to cut me open and remove whatever was causing this.

The emergency room immediately took me into the back

and began X-rays after injecting me with dye. I lay there in agony for about an hour before they determined that I had a kidney stone and gave me a shot of morphine. I could not tell that it had any effect at all until they tried to move me from the gurney to a wheelchair. I was sure I could do it myself, but my legs had turned to rubber. I was in the hospital two days before I passed the stone and they released me. The doctor said kidney stones and childbirth were the two most painful things there were.

The nurse said, "I've had both. Kidney stones are worse, at least with childbirth you get something for your trouble."

All my effort of controlling my liquid intake had backfired. Someone should have warned me. As I was leaving the hospital, they gave me a pitcher for my desk at school and told me to empty it every day.

I received a lot of 'welcome backs' as I stood by my classroom door when the students entered the next morning. I walked over to my desk and found several 'get well' messages. One stood out.

Mr. Williams.

I hope you get well soon. We HATE this substitute, so get back soon. She won't even make any jokes, she won't even let us laugh!!! Never let her substitute again.

There was also a cassette tape with 'From Athena to Mr. Williams' written on it. The short message on the tape said that Athena, the Goddess of Wisdom, had been watching me for a while and was hoping a man like me would come along. She hoped that one day I would live on Mt. Olympus with the other Greek gods. Until then I should continue what I am doing and keep up the good work.

My all too brief moment of reverie ended when a student called out,

"Mr. Williams, Arnold just peed in the soap dispenser!"

Soap dispensers were attached to the walls in the restrooms. They were easily refillable by twisting them so the screwable container was on the bottom. That is how Fred said Arnold did it.

Arnold, of course, denied it. I believed Fred but did not

see it with my own eyes and there were no other witnesses. Nothing could be done but talking to Fred. That is how justice worked in elementary schools.

Our new principal, Mrs. Harris, not only believed in the phrase, '*a person who feels appreciated will always do more than expected,*' but put it into practice. It seemed to be her superpower. Having said that, not all of her comments were glowing compliments.

"You do a great job with your Greek unit and I know the kids like it," she said. "I've even gotten a few compliments from parents about how much their kids talk about your class. I hate to be the bearer of bad news, but I've gotten a few complaints too. Public schools are neutral on religion and some parents have complained that if their god can't be taught, no gods should be taught. They're objecting to you teaching about the Greek gods."

"You're kidding!"

"I wish that was the case. Not all of those complaints were from parents. One was from a preacher. The school board wants to avoid any controversy."

"In other words, they're spineless."

"Well, that's one way to look at it. I'm afraid you're on the religious right's hitlist."

"What does that mean?"

"You don't have to stop your Greek lessons, and you can still dress up in that outfit, but you have to stop telling stories about the Greek gods for a while. It also means they're going to monitor what you teach and complain to the school board about anything they don't like. Anything at all. I just want to warn you to be aware. Here's a list of things they object to."

Mrs. Harris gave me a mimeographed brochure for parents telling them not to allow their children to participate in classroom discussions of values, classroom discussions of the future, writing autobiographies or family histories, writing about their own values or feelings, taking intelligence tests, to participate in role-playing activities, and finally, never to confide in teachers, especially social studies or English teachers. It tells parents to put their complaints in writing, send documented complaints to the media, and make complaints widely known.

The next day I saw something in my homeroom class that

I was sure the religious right would object to. A bushy-haired blond boy was wearing earrings. An even bigger surprise was that no one in the room seemed to notice but me.

I quietly asked Joey to take them off and he did.

Joey Blair was a good kid, so I was surprised to see him wearing the earrings again when he came into my third period social studies class. Again I told him to take them off and again he did. I asked him to step into the hallway so we could talk in private after I saw him wearing them a third time before the end of the period.

"What's going on, Joey?"

"I'm not very good at sports, and I'm not very good at school, but my mom says I'm good at looking good."

It was all for attention and was not disturbing anyone. In fact, the other kids did not even seem to notice. I did not think I could deal with him and handle my social studies class at the same time, so I sent him to see the guidance counselor. I never saw him wearing earrings again, but he started wearing a gold chain around his neck and an ID bracelet on his wrist. For a while he even wore a fuzzy scarf around his neck even though the weather was much too warm for it.

I forgot to bring my lunch from home that day and the cafeteria was serving fish. Even though I lived in Florida, the only seafood I liked was shrimp and scallops. I hoped no one else could hear my stomach rumbling, though I certainly did.

As soon as I walk into my apartment, I opened my refrigerator to figure out what to have for dinner when my phone rang.

It was a mother calling to ask how her son was doing in school. My phone number was on the Princsonia parents' grapevine (an informal network for school gossip). Seeing over a hundred and fifty students a day, my memory for names was not the best. I did not recognize the name she gave me, but luckily I had my grade book nearby. Quickly flipping through the pages, I scanned all five periods and did not see the name she told me.

"Which period is he in?" I asked.

"What do you mean, which period is he in? He's in your room all day."

"None of my students are in my room all day. We

change classes in the sixth grade."

"Sixth grade! My son is a fifth grader."

"That explains why I can't find him in my grade book."

"But he has to be in your class. You're the only teacher he talks about."

"Maybe he's got a friend in my room, or maybe he's just excited about our Greek Day. He'll be in my class next year if he still goes to Princsonia."

I hung up feeling flattered but also puzzled that a parent did not know who her own son's teacher was.

Experience has taught me the importance of modesty in the classroom. I used to say, "I think I'm a fair teacher," and a little voice in the back of the room would always mumble, "no you're not." I eventually switched to saying, "I never said I was fair," and the little voice said, "yes you are." That always sounded a lot nicer.

After giving my class an assignment to work on, I sat at my desk.

Edward De Luca walked up to my desk and asked, "Mr. Williams, do you know why I like you?"

"No, why?"

"I don't know either, but I do."

Edward was very bright and always completed his assignments quickly. He frequently came up to my desk asking if there was anything he could do to help me. His elderly looking father said Edward had a thyroid problem that made him hyperactive but he was able to channel it in a positive way. He also told me in confidence that he was really Edward's grandfather, and the woman Edward thought was his older sister, was actually his mother.

One day after completing a messy chore for me, he walked over to the sink and picked up what he thought was powdered soap and began washing his hands and arms. He gave a sudden loud shriek when he realized that the goo on his arms was blue tempera paint.

Marie McGuinness, the language arts teacher, walked into my classroom before school one morning to ask, "Have you noticed those fortune teller signs with the big hand on it? Have you ever wondered what goes on in one of those places?"

"Well, good morning to you too."

"Sorry, good morning. I pass one of those places every day driving to school. I'm curious about what it would be like to go there, but I'm afraid to go by myself. I was wondering if you might be interested in going there with me. Are you free after school today?"

"Today I'm meeting a friend for dinner and we're going to see a movie. I'm free tomorrow, but how much is this going to cost me?"

"I think a reading is $20, and if you really hate it, I'll give your money back."

"OK, I guess so," I said reluctantly, wondering what I had gotten myself into.

As much as I wanted there to be a way to know my good days and bad days in advance, and who I should trust or love, and who I should not, I did not believe anything like that existed. I did not believe in fate, karma, horoscopes, or any 'divine plan' for our lives. I did not believe in the supernatural in any shape or form. Except for humans making things happen, most of life was made up of meaningless random events that happened for no rhyme or reason.

Marie and I drove separately. As I drove, I recalled two times that I had premonitions. As I was going to Princsonia Elementary for the first time, I imagined that things would go well if I was given room 12. I was given room 12. Another time I went to a job interview and imagined if there were three interviewers, I would get the job. There were three, but I did not get the job.

I pulled into the parking lot with the big sign announcing Madam May, Fortune Teller, and saw Marie sitting in her car waiting for me.

She was nervous and asked me to go in first.

I walked toward the door wondering if Madam May would be using a crystal ball and maybe some incense.

I paid the twenty dollars and was shown into a room where I was left alone to absorb the atmosphere. The small room had a simple table and two chairs. Religious pictures hung on the walls and a single candle burned on the table.

Madam May genuflected and crossed herself as she entered the room and took a seat across from me.

"Put out your hand, palm up," she instructed.

She gently grasped my hand as she stared into space over my head for nearly a minute before she started talking. She spoke in vague general terms with very few specifics.

When the session was over, I sat in my car waiting while Marie went in.

She came out about twenty minutes later. The fortune teller must not have known we were together because she told both of us exactly the same things.

Both of us were told we had had two or three near death experiences, but they were behind us now. The second half of our lives will be better than the first half. People appear to like us to our face, but do not really like us behind our back. Both of us were going to marry within two years. We will never be rich but also never be poor and we will both live a long, happy, healthy life.

The next day the other teachers wanted to know what we had been told. Nearly all of them thought we should go to another fortune teller for a second opinion.

Weather in Florida can be unpredictable. Anyone who has lived here very long has seen it rain in the front yard but not in the back yard. It was sunny as I drove to school, but, less than two hours later, the sky turned dark gray and it started raining.

One of the students noticed a drip coming from the over-head air-conditioner.

I walked over to see what was going on and was suddenly drenched by a four-foot wide wall of water that burst out of it.

"Donna, go get one of the janitors, quick!"

Soon my entire classroom floor was under water and it was spreading out to the hallway.

My students were divided up among the other four teachers and I was sent home for the day to change clothes.

Since nothing like that had ever happened before, Mrs. Harris thought it was just a freak happening. When it happened a second time, maintenance men from the school board office came to check it out. The school's roof had recently been resurfaced and two of the drains over my classroom had been clogged up with tar.

Even though our classroom air-conditioner produced both stink bombs and a waterfall, in Florida it was still better to have one than not.

One of my students, Cindy Salyer, was unusually giggly. Girls love to tell on each other and told me that Cindy found a small bottle of vodka at her bus stop and drank it. I am not sure whether she was really drunk or whether she just thought that was how she was supposed to act. Her parents were called and they had to deal with it.

The school secretary came to my door saying two students went home that day with lice, so all students needed to be checked. That was not really a surprise since one or two lice outbreaks a year was common. Students found with lice were sent home and not allowed to return unless someone from the Health Department or their doctor certified that they were lice free. The school nurse normally did the checks but was absent that day. We needed to check the students' hair ourselves. The secretary gave us rubber gloves and a fine-toothed comb.

"But I don't have a clue what lice even look like."

"Look for dandruff that moves, or tiny eggs that don't. They're called nits."

I had the class get in a line and I went through their hair one child at a time. I kept imagining people asking me what I did for a living, 'Oh, I'm a lice inspector, and at the risk of sounding nit-picky, business is lousy.'

It happened often enough that I started keeping one or two bottles of lice shampoo at home just for days like today.

Mrs. McGuinness said we needed to go to another fortune teller to get second opinions. I thought the whole idea was a joke but agreed. I phoned a fortune teller in a nearby town and made an appointment. She told me to bring a spool of thread and an old handkerchief.

I arrived at her large expensive looking house at eleven o'clock Sunday morning. Again I was shown to a small room with religious pictures on the wall, lit with a single candle.

"Did you bring the thread and handkerchief?" asked Madam June.

"Yes, I have them right here."

As she talked, she cut the thread into about fifty three-inch strands. Madam June held the bundle out to me asking me to pick just one and tie a knot in it. She wound it up into a ball, placing it in the palm of her left hand.

"I'm going to pray to ask god if he wants me to help you.

If not, you are to go away and come back one year and one day from today and I'll ask again. If god does want me to help you, he'll untie the knot in this thread."

She closed her hand and said a silent prayer. She crossed herself and opened her hand, shouting "Hallelujah!"

I jumped from surprise.

"You came to the right place. God does want me to help you!"

She told me almost word for word what the first fortune teller said. Then she asked if there were any problems I needed help with. When I said no, she asked if I would like more money.

She took scissors and cut my old handkerchief into about a five or six-inch square and told me to put three high denomination bills, the higher the better, in the center and showed me how to fold it. I was told to pin it to the inside my underwear and wear it next to my skin for five days. Then I was to return to her with the money. She would say a prayer over it and donate it to her church. God would bless it and return it to me several times over.

I told her I understood and drove away, grateful that it had not cost me more than twenty dollars. It was worth that much just for the theater of it. I may be dumb but I am not stupid.

Of course there are exceptions, but most girls begin sixth grade with chests indistinguishable from the boys. This is the age when most begin wearing training bras. One day they are flat chested and appear to have boobs the next. Sharon Humbard was the exception. Only eleven, she had more in her blouse than most of the teachers. The boys noticed. Sharon seemed to enjoy the attention until one day she got a note saying, 'Herman wants to F__k you.' She did not say a word about it to any adult at school but took it home to show her mother.

The next morning Mrs. Humbard, her mother, stopped two police officers and told them to follow her to school because there was going to be trouble.

She yelled at the principal and insisted on seeing Herman face-to-face. The mother wanted Herman arrested or at least suspended for a month.

Mrs. Harris wisely refused. The note said, 'Herman

wants to….' not 'I want to…' so he probably did not even write the note.

I doubt the note was the real problem. I think the real problem was that Herman was black. If the note had come from a white boy, I doubt Sharon would have minded at all.

Sharon always seemed to have ten and twenty-dollar bills with her. That was unusual in the sixth grade. Other students said Sharon's mother was a waitress at a truck stop and would give her money if she was 'nice' to the truckers.

Several students invited me to watch their Little League or soccer games in the evenings or weekends. The parents seemed to appreciate it when I came.

I sat in the bleachers at a softball game when one of my students sat down beside me. He looked up into the sky and said he thought it might rain.

I opened my mouth to reply, and he said,

"Oh no, now I've done it. Here comes a lecture on where rain comes from!"

I got the message loud and clear and did not say another word until the game was over.

A few days later on Saturday, I found myself standing beside a soccer field watching another student play. After her game, she joined me at the sidelines chatting while I waited to watch another student play in the third game scheduled for that morning.

One player in the second game was clearly more outstanding than the other players on the field. I am not a sports fan so don't have the knowledge to know why he was so outstanding, but I did notice that the heads of all the other players bounced up and down as they ran. Instead of bouncing, the outstanding player's head seemed to float smoothly.

My student standing next to me did not like my comments because I was supposed to be cheering for my own students and not paying attention to someone neither of us even knew.

On Monday morning the intercom summoned us to the library. Usually faculty meetings were announced a week or more in advance. Mrs. Harris told us we had to empty our closets, take every book off our shelves, and remove everything from our cabinets because the school board office was sending out a team of workers to paint our school.

We asked why it could not wait until summer break.

"There's too many schools in the county to paint them all over the summers, plus they don't want to air-condition an entire school just for the painting crew. Instead they spend their summers painting the exteriors of schools."

It was like living in a bad dream for two weeks. Walls were stripped, and books, papers, equipment, and furniture, were piled on the floor in the center of the room. A hurricane could not have done a messier job.

While all this was going on, we still had to teach our classes. When the painters were working in our room, we had to move our class to the cafeteria, stage, library, or outside under a tree. Because classes were being held in the cafeteria, we had to eat lunch in our cluttered classrooms. A few kids even got sick from the paint fumes.

Paint seemed to jump off the walls. Every day two or three kids would get drops of paint on their clothes just walking in the hallways. Luckily the office could take care of that as long as they got to it before the paint dried.

The sixth grade was having three or four parent conferences each week. I usually hated them except when parents said their kids talked about my class all the time.

"It's always Mr. Williams said this, or Mr. Williams said that."

Several of our meetings were a little strange, but one stood out as especially odd. Parents asked us to stop girls from phoning their son in the evenings after he had gone to bed. They were uncomfortable mentioning it to the girls' parents themselves because they socialized with them and thought it could be awkward.

They were not happy with our answer when we explained that we have no control over what students did in their own homes.

One day in class, one of my students was bragging about how strong he was.

"Oh you think so, do you?" I said. "I challenge you to stand up and hold your arms out, shoulder level, for five minutes."

About half the kids took the challenge, and I became the

timekeeper.

Around the three-minute point kids started giving up and sat down. Only one student made it the full five minutes.

"Wow! I'm impressed." I said. "You must have been hypnotized."

The next morning before school, the mother of one of my students came into my room to thank me for teaching hypnotism and witchcraft. She and her daughter were practicing witches and thought it was about time that it was recognized by the school.

I was forced to explain that her daughter misunderstood what had happened.

The mother did not appear to be much smarter than her daughter and did not seem to understand what I was saying. I failed to understand any link between hypnosis and witchcraft (except that I did not believe in either), but she clearly saw it and left my room still singing my praises.

Even though I was a sixth grade teacher, I often encountered younger students in the hallways, library, and playground. Sometimes I love to mess with their minds. One day a first grade girl came up to me and said,

"My sister is in your room. She says you're funny."

"My sister? I don't have a sister."

"No, my sister, me!"

"Oh, I see the problem now, you're pointing to yourself and saying me. You're not me, I'm me. You're you."

"No, I'm me."

"No, I'm pretty sure I'm me. I'm a lot older than you and I was me way before you were ever born."

"No, I'm me!"

"How can both of us be me? Now that sounds a little silly doesn't it? Let's try something else. We're both standing here, right?"

She nodded.

"OK, I'm going to walk over there."

I walked about ten feet and asked,

"Did I walk over there?"

"Yes," said the first grader.

"No, I didn't. I walked here, *you* are there. Here and there. You really are confused, but I'm sure you'll figure it out one day."

I walked away leaving a very puzzled look on her face.

It was a frequent conversation that I had with several of the younger students.

Working in an elementary school is definitely a woman's world. If men wonder what women talk about, I know. They mostly talk about their families, and who is dating who. They occasionally talk about their favorite male celebrities, restaurants or vacation spots they have been to or want to go to. They talk a lot less about cooking and fashion than I expected, with one exception. I was surprised at how often they talked about bra sizes. I did not go into the teachers' lounge very often, but when I did, they would often noticeably change the subject. By the end of my second year at Princsonia, I could walk into the lounge and they would continue their conversation without even a hint of a pause. That is when I knew I had been accepted as one of the herd.

One morning before the bell rang, a student ran into my room, yelling, "Mr. Williams, there's a fight on the playground!"

This was not news any teacher wanted to hear. It was even less welcome because the end of the year was approaching so soon.

Two girls were fighting, and one was holding a pair of scissors - not the ones with the rounded ends, but pointy scissors. A group of kids surrounded them yelling encouragement. The playground supervisor was already there, but she was cautious about getting hurt herself. Without thinking, I grabbed the wrist holding the scissors and stepped between the two girls. I knew she was not mad at me, so I did not feel threatened. The girl behind me accidentally ripped my shirt trying to shove me out of the way. The sound of my shirt ripping startled both girls and the fight came to a halt. I marched both girls to the office, and they were suspended for two weeks.

I returned to my classroom to receive a round of applause from my students. They regarded me as a hero, but that was not the image I wanted. I am much more of a nerd and proud of it.

Some of my girls told me that Monica Jordan had marijuana at school. It was the last week of school before summer break and my hopes of a quiet week were shattered.

I asked Monica to show it to me and without hesitation she pulled a small packet of seeds out of her purse. I had no idea what marijuana looked like so sent them to the office. No one there knew either, so the police were called.

The seeds really were marijuana. Monica claimed someone gave her a used purse and the seeds were already inside. That is possible I supposed, but how did she know what they were? I didn't.

EIGHT

STUDENT EVALUATIONS WRITTEN IN MRS.

McGUINNESS' CLASS

My Year In The Sixth Grade

If I would ever remember all the mischief and trouble I
caused this would be some monotonous report, or whatever you
call it. The food was lousy, I always used to bring my lunch.
The food was indigestible and the milk was mostly sour. But
once in a blue moon they gave out a good lunch. And when they
did, I never bought it that day. So much for the lunch bit. Now
I'll tell you a little bit about my teachers. First there was Mr.

Williams. He was so awkward and funny. He wore those weird glasses and once a month he'd shave. Then he barely matched his clothes. He looked like a lighted Christmas tree. Although, he was nice and my homeroom teacher. Well he was easy going and the year passed by surprisingly fast. Next there was Mrs. McGuinness. She was nice too. And always determined to teach us more. She thought the most of us. She was always telling us what we would have to learn. When she got mad she made us take out these sorry dictionaries and write the one thousand and one definitions of the word 'order.' There was Mrs. Tilton. She was often mean. She piled us up with homework. Oh my! Such strenuous work it was! And the precious hours I used when I could be sleeping. But the thing that I hated the most was P.E. I used to hate doing all those exercises, which corroded my muscles with pain. Well there you have it. Gosh that's not even the half of it.

My Year In The 6th Grade

I really enjoyed my social studies class. The main thing I liked about it is the teacher because he is so nice. He was fun to be with almost all the time. The country that I don't think I will ever forget is Ancient Greece. I really liked learning about it and wished we could have stayed on it longer. I also enjoyed New Zealand. The thing that I think was the most boring was when we watched films. I would much rather hear Mr. Williams talk about different things. I had a lot of interest in his class because it was more fun to learn in there, I don't think I want to leave Mr. Williams. His class is my favorite and he is my favorite teacher. Even though he did get mad at times, I still like him.

I was very flattered by what most of the kids wrote about me, so decided to give my own class evaluation.

I asked the students to answer the following questions:

1.   What do you like most about this class?

2.   What do you like least about this class?

3.   How would you change this class?

4.   What have you learned the most about in this class?

5.   What would you most like to learn in this class?

6.   Do you have any addition comments to make about this class?

1. What do you like most about this class?

A. Mr. Williams, the way he makes you laugh, he can just look at you and you will laugh.

B. The way you don't always teach from a book.

C. I have a lot of friends in it.

D. It has a good pencil sharpener.

E. The seating arrangement.

F. We learned about Greece and I did not know that much of it.

G. There is only 25 more days of it.

2. What did you like least about this class?

A. When you whisper you get a report to write.

B. It smells, but everything else is OK.

C. Your dry jokes.

D. When everyone is quiet.

E. The smell that comes from the air-conditioner.

F. The people, because they don't treat some people right.

G. Greeks

H. Doing reports

I. The air-conditioner

J. My teacher, sometimes when he does not be mad, I love him, but I like him best when he isn't here.

3. How would you change this class?

A. Kick the teacher out and play all day.

B. Put more Blacks in the class.

C. When you get in trouble you should have to kiss a girl.

D. The teacher's looks.

E. Let us talk more

F. By letting me be the teacher

G. By making the teacher uglier and purple so we can have more fun.

H. Get a new air-conditioner.

I. I wouldn't because I really love all my teachers to the tip of my heart, that is if I have one. Anyway, what's wrong with this class?

J. Get the bad people out.

K. I would put in a new air-conditioner cause it just don't work.

4. What have you learned the most about in this class?

   A. Mostly about Greece.

   B. The Middle Ages.

   C. I have learned all the insults Mr. Williams uses.

   D. Greece

   E. Not to talk out loud.

   F. Rome.

   G. Foreign countries.

   H. Ancient Greece

   I. States, countries, cities, and people.

5. What would you like to learn in this class?

A. Art.

B. Paraguay

C. How to make money the easy way

D. Hitler

E. The martial arts

F. Liquid embroidery

G. I don't kwite know.

H. How to kiss a boy like Bob.

I. None of your business

J. Computers

K. Sex

6. Do you have any additional comments to make about this class?

The think I enjoyed most about your class was because you were so funny. I am not going to write a lot because you know about the things I believe in. That's another thing, I liked you because whenever my day went bad and I was worrying, I always knew I could talk to you about it. I do not know why I can talk to you about all my problems when I can't even tall my own Dad. But there is just a special feeling that I have that makes me feel comfortable when I talk to you. This may or may not be what you wanted to hear, but I just thought I would tell you my feelings cause like I said I have always felt comfortable when I have talked with you, and I hope to see you again.

I think Mr. Williams can get through to anyone he wants. He has different methods of unlocking feelings. (1) He has a question box which he lets people put notes into. (2) He cracks jokes or teases us about things. One day I'll never forget. You told us something that startled me. It was when you told what

the "Greek gym suit" was.

Dear Mr. Williams,

My year was very nice because I always had a funny class to go to. They ought to let Mrs. Hazen smoke in class because she gets nervous and when she gets nervous, she yells a lot. I like Mrs. McGuinness because she don't give no homework.

NINE

Each year had its own kind of crazy, but on the whole I liked my job and felt it was important. On the other hand, who doesn't think vacations are better than work? Both the calendar and my bank account said it was time to go back to work even though both my mind and body were resisting.

The longer I taught, the more I loved Ancient Greece. I spent a lot of my income buying books, pictures, furniture, and copies of ancient pottery and statues. My home was starting to resemble a Greek museum.

I was sure I was still on the religious right's hit list, but I believed I moved down a few notches. Now they grumbled about Christmas and Easter Break being renamed Winter and Spring Break. It was done out of respect for other religions, but they declared that Christianity itself was under attack. They claimed America would be better if prayers and the Bible were put back into schools. Prayers were NEVER taken out of schools. They just can no longer be led by school personnel. Students have always been free to pray privately in school anytime they want. Even the Bible praises praying in private (Matthew 6:6).

Every year the PTA had a 'Welcome Back' social so they could get to know the teachers, and to find out how we wanted them to help the school. I always found them awkward and felt like we were on display. The itinerant band teacher transferred from Kenwood to Princsonia. Richard Freeman and I were only acquaintances, but it was nice to see him again.

"Several of the teachers here don't believe the stories I tell about Kenwood."

"Can you blame them? My friends and family don't believe my stories either. One of the schools where I taught had some expensive amplifiers that were just left out in the hallway for about two years with no problems. The amplifiers were moved into a locked closet and were stolen a few days later. No one knew they were valuable until they were locked up."

"The best way to hide something from those kids would be to put it in a book," I added. "They'd never think of looking there."

"I don't expect a beginning band class to know much about music, but the first time I had my intermediate class play something, they weren't even playing the same song. I went up to one kid and pointed to his music book. 'Just play the notes,' I told him. The boy looked up at me and said, 'So that's a note!' The high school band isn't much better. The only formation they can make during halftime is a period, and they could only do that on a good day. The people in the bleachers didn't recognize the song they played, but the drums were nice and loud."

"To be fair, there were some nice kids there," I added.

"True, but too many of them are addlepated and it brings the average down."

Unfortunately, most of the students at Kenwood - and their parents - placed a low value on education and it was reflected in both their attitude and behavior.

A major shift happened in public schools thanks to the federal No Child Left Behind law. A statewide test, called the FCAT (Florida Comprehensive Assessment Test) changed what and how teachers taught. Reading, Math, and Science became the focus with specific benchmarks and standards. Social studies was not on the test, so I was told to emphasize reading skills much more than historical facts. Cursive, penmanship, art, and music were downgraded because they were not on the test. Teaching for the test became all important. Sadly, instead of being regarded as people with individual personalities, students were reduced to being little more than test scores.

One of my students was born in Cannes, France. I was pleased because it gave me a chance to try out my junior high school French.

"Bonjour! Je m'appelle, Mr. Williams. Je suis professeur."

"I know English some," she said in a heavy accent.

Her name was Micheline Belanger (Bell-on-zjay), which I believe is the most beautiful name I have ever heard. She always looked very serious. I wondered if that was because she was in a strange school surrounded by strangers, or if the French took a serious approach to school, or if that was just her personality. Micheline's parents divorced a few years ago and her American father returned to Florida to open a wine shop. She came here to live with her father over the summer so she could learn to speak English fluently. Her mother remained in Cannes.

As usual, my first social studies class began by turning off the classroom lights and holding up the globe in front of the overhead projector to show how it could be both day and night at the same time. My first homework assignment was for the students to write out the definitions of: city, county, state, country, and continent.

This was my fifth year of teaching and by now had received a variety of excuses on why kids do not have their homework:

I forgot it at home.

My dog ate it.

It's in my homeroom.

It's in the car.

I don't know.

My dog spilt tea on mine.

I lost it.

I ate it.

My dog had an accident on it.

Tony never gave it back to me.

I didn't do it.

Oh, dear!

To tell you the truth, I just don't know where it went to.

I left it on the bus.

Mom washed it in the washing machine.

What homework?

It was Saturday morning and I was in a clothing store at the mall. I had just picked up a 3-pack of boxer briefs when I heard,

"Hello Mr. Williams," called Kwame Wilson, one of my students. "I didn't expect to see you here."

I quickly put the underwear back on the shelf and took a step away.

"What are you doing?"

"The same as everyone else, just looking around to see if there's anything I want."

"It seems strange to see you outside of school."

"Teachers are real people. We do the same things other people do."

"If you say so. See you on Monday."

I spent the rest of my visit to the mall looking over my shoulder to see who might be watching.

The most unusual thing to happen on Monday came to my attention when the P.E. teacher called me aside to talk in private when I picked up my students from the playground.

"I think you need to have a talk with Chris Conley about appropriate behavior at school. I didn't see it, but the other kids said he kissed Joey Harper. I know Joey can be a bully at times, but it really freaked him out."

I called the redhead into the hall when we got back to our room.

"So what's this I hear about you kissing Joey?"

"Joey and I got into an argument. I was afraid he was going to hit me, so I kissed him to scare him away."

"Did it work?"

"Yes."

We went back into the room to find a red-faced Joey wanting the whole thing to go away.

It was all I could manage to hold back a chuckle.

After a bathroom break, we changed classes.

Standing in front of a map of Africa, I tried to give the same introduction to Ancient Egypt to all five of my classes.

"People were living in the Nile River Valley before 5,000 B.C. The area was a desert. Rain was rare and the land was hot and dry. Egypt was called 'The Gift of the Nile' because every year the Nile River flooded and left behind a rich fertile layer of black soil that was good for their crops. The river also gave them…"

"Eric Berger, your lunch is in the office," blared the intercom.

"As I was saying, before I was so rudely interrupted, the

river also gave them drinking water and irrigation for their fields. The farmers lived in small villages, and each village had its own leader. The leaders fought with each other for control of more land. Eventually the delta area, Lower Egypt, was united under one leader, and Upper Egypt was united under another leader. Around 3000 B.C., one man..."

"Would Gary and Brian Applegate report to the office. Bring your things because you'll be going home," interrupted the intercom.

"Both Upper and Lower Egypt were united by King Menes, also called Narmer. Some people think they were the same man, other people think they were father and son."

I muddled through the rest of my introduction, but the intercom destroyed my concentration. Princsonia's new school secretary seemed to love making announcements.

It happened way too often. I was annoyed and couldn't wait for the weekend.

At home that weekend, I saw a funny picture on the internet showing a sleeping cat covered with small cheese flavored crackers. The words suggested trying it to see how many you could put on a cat before it woke up. I was in a silly mood and printed up three copies.

On Monday morning, I quietly taped one next to the cafeteria door, another over a water fountain in the hall, and the third next to the library door.

I overheard the kids laughing.

That was a mistake. Getting a deliberate laugh only encourages me to do it again.

The next morning, I replaced all three signs with 'WARNING, Dry Paint!'

This was my third year at Princsonia and I was gaining a reputation as a jokester. Several students came up to me asking if I put up the signs. I just played dumb, I'm good at that.

"What pictures? What are you talking about? Why would you think I would do something like that?"

I found another picture on the internet of a cat lying under three or four remote controls, and the caption read, 'This Isn't Even REMOTEly Funny."

--- more laughter and more questions about whether I did it ---

The next morning, I replaced those signs with two other

signs, 'Do NOT Read This Sign' and 'It Is OK To Read This Sign.'

On Friday morning of the following week, I was seen by a student, Maria Agullo, as I taped up a sign that said, 'Florida State Law Prohibits Underwater Smoking On School Property.'

After two weeks, my secret was out. I stopped hanging the posters, and in just a few days the kids were begging me to start again. I did, but only hung them in my classroom and only replaced them once a week instead of daily.

Not everything was so frivolous. At first I was very skeptical of the 'hyperactivity' diagnosis, thinking it was just an excuse for bad behavior. Time and experience made me a believer. No teacher should be allowed into a classroom without taking a course in behavior disorders that will probably be encountered, such as, hyperactivity, dyslexia, autism, Asperger's, Tourette's Syndrome, etc.

James Hagee was diagnosed with hyperactivity and prescribed medicine to control it, but his mother refused to let him take it because it made him feel sluggish. One day coming back from the cafeteria he felt energetic and started turning cartwheels crashing into other kids. Another day, also coming back from the cafeteria, he started swinging his arms in excitement and hit both the kid in front and behind him. He had a very kind soul and did not want to bother anyone but frequently and unintentionally did. His hyperactivity made him act spontaneously without thinking ahead of the consequences. One day he kicked a ball into a crowd of people and was surprised when it hit anyone. All he thought about was kicking the ball never considering where it might go. James was a well-intentioned troublemaker.

As usual, I was standing at the entrance of my classroom Monday morning as the students entered.

Tommy Bain said, "Saturday was my birthday and I had a big party."

"I know what you did Saturday night, Mr. Williams," said Sara Wilson. "You had dinner at the Purple Pickle with a woman. Is she your girlfriend? Are you going to marry her?"

"How do you know where I ate? I didn't see anyone there that I knew?"

"I have my ways," she answered.

"Pete and I saw you at Publix last week."

This was getting ridiculous. I could not set foot outside my house without my students knowing where I went, what I did, who I was with, and even what I ate.

As we sat around the teacher's table at lunch later that day, Mrs. McGuinness announced, "Joan Frazier is sitting in the office for shooting the moon in my class."

"But Joan is gifted!" said one teacher.

"Gifted kids have butts too," I added.

"What are you talking about?" asked Mrs. Hazen. "What does shooting the moon mean?"

"Joan and another girl got into an argument and Joan dropped her pants and flashed her bare bottom," explained Mrs. McGuinness. "It's considered an insult."

"I've never heard that term before," said Mrs. Hazen. "If one of my students told me someone had shot the moon, I would have said, 'That's nice.'"

Mrs. Tilton would have been pleased if she had known that the No Child Left Behind Act was requiring me to do fewer fun projects and give more reading assignments. I do not know if that was the intent of the federal legislators who passed it, but that is how our school system implemented it.

Unfortunately, too many people look back on their social studies class with less than fondness. It is fully understandable because too many social studies teachers just told their students to read the chapter and answer the questions at the end. Textbook authors try to avoid controversy, so the books are extremely boring. We have all read many long passages in social studies books that don't say anything.

I gave a reading assignment and took another student into the hall to give a private answer to a note he put in the question box. When we stepped back into the class, I noted that a girl had put her head on her desk and was sound asleep. A student falling asleep in my class had only happened one time before. That time I bumped his desk, and he jumped up suddenly wide awake. This time I had another idea. I quietly told all the other students to silently step into the hall. I turned off the lights and loudly closed the door. The girl suddenly woke up and ran out into the hall in panic. Since the room was empty and the lights were off, she thought school was over and she had missed her bus. She never fell asleep in my room again.

Not only were readings from the social studies textbook boring for the students, they were boring for me as well. For my own amusement I wrote notes and randomly slipped them into pages we would read that day.

You can't read this note without smiling!

Wave at Mr. Williams.

Smile if you think Mr. Williams is funny (looking).

Isn't reading this book better than listening to Mr. Williams talk?
(I loved it when the kids nodded NO)

Sometimes I would stage a treasure hunt by handing a note to a student who I thought needed some encouragement. The first note might say, 'Look up the word GREECE in the dictionary on Mr. Williams' desk." That revealed a note saying,

'Look under the globe.' There would be ten or twelve such notes leading to a piece of hard candy.

I read an article on the importance of background music so occasionally I would play pop or classical music while the students read or worked on assignments. We often clashed on musical tastes and from time to time a student would ask,

"Why are you punishing us?"

"OK, if you don't like my music, I'll turn it off," I would reply.

Even though they didn't like my music, it was preferable to silence.

After attending a Michael Feinstein concert, I brought in one of his CDs, "Pure Gershwin."

My students didn't care for most of the songs but did like "Let's Call the Whole Thing Off," and often sang along with the chorus. The song muses about a romantic relationship between an upper-class woman and a middle-class man.

"You like potato and I like potatoe, you like tomato and I like tomatoe,....."

At one of our sixth grade meetings I told the other

teachers that I had received a Jury Summons in the mail and would be missing a day or more of school.

"Some lawyers don't like teachers," said Mrs. Hazen, "because we usually take the side of the cops."

When the day arrived, I checked into the jury room and sat in a room with two or three hundred other people. We were shown a fifteen-minute video on the importance of jury duty and waited to be called. I was in the first group of twenty-five people sent to a courtroom.

"This case is about the defendant being accused of attacking a policeman," one of the lawyers informed us.

We were all asked general questions, such as, do you know anyone involved in this case, can you be fair and objective, has anyone in your close family been accused of assault, etc. Then we were asked individual questions.

"Mr. Williams, the questionnaire you filled out says you're a teacher. What grade?"

"Sixth."

"How would you handle a student hitting another student that you didn't actually see yourself?"

"I would ask other students in the area to step out into the hall, one at a time, and ask what they saw."

"Why would you ask them to step into the hall?" asked the defense attorney.

"Because they are more likely to tell the truth. They don't want to look like a tattle-tale in front of the others," I answered. "It's considered squealing. Sixth graders don't mind telling but don't want to be seen doing it."

I was dismissed back to the jury room, while I assumed the attorney moved on the question other potential jury members.

Except for that brief courtroom visit, it was a long boring day of waiting before we were dismissed around noon. I wish I had thought to bring something to read.

Technology replaced our grade books. We now took attendance and kept grades on a computer in each classroom. Lesson plans were also written online but still had to be printed out and stapled into our lesson plan book so substitutes could easily find them. Every computer was connected to a server or bank of servers, so the principal could look at anyone's grades or lesson plans whenever he or she wished.

Unlike the other teachers, I loved computers and thought it was great, but it did make it harder to boost a student's grade. I have never lowered a student's grade but if I thought the student was making an effort, sometimes I would boost a D to a C, and occasionally a C to a B to encourage them. Shhh, do not tell anyone I did that.

I found a thin spiral notebook in my office mailbox with a sticky note that said,

'You need to read this. I ask the students to keep a journal of their thoughts and feelings. This is a huge weight for a young person to have to carry around. It's heartbreaking.'

I opened Micheline's notebook to the bookmarked page.

When I live in France, I miss my father. When I live here, I miss my mother. I wonder if I will ever be happy again. Maybe if I lived in the middle of the Atlantic Ocean, I would be closer to both of them.

When most students are accused of breaking a school rule, they react by denying it. Not Zachary Pappas. With a big smile on his face – there was always a big smile on Zack's face – he would look you right in the eye, put an arm around your back, and gush out, "I'm sorry. I'll try to do better next time." Sometimes he would apologize for things I did not even know about yet. Happy, bubbly, likeable, charming, and charismatic were all words that described Zack. He liked everyone and everyone liked him. He had no ill will toward anyone and would do almost anything to get a laugh. He frequently brought whoopee cushions, disappearing ink, extra-hot mints, electric shock pens, and other toys to school. I wish I could give just a little of Zack's exuberance to Micheline.

The music teacher walked into my classroom before school one day.

"Good morning, I have a favor to ask and before you say no, it involves a substitute and getting away from school for a few hours."

"You've got my attention, go on."

"I need another faculty member to co-chair the Princsonia

Service Club. You'd actually be more of a chaperone. Three or four times a year I take the school chorus to a few nursing homes in the area to sing for the residents. It's an easy job and I'm asking you because I know you like photography and want you to take pictures."

"That's all you want me to do, take pictures?"

"And also help watch the kids, but these are chorus kids. They're not behavior problems."

"OK, I'll give it a try."

Besides teaching the students songs, Mrs. Woodruff also taught them how to make simple dolls out of yarn to give the elderly nursing home patients.

Our first trip was a success, but I was not prepared for how emotional the residents became. It was clear that a few had no idea what was going on or even where they were. Most of them were so overcome with joy from our visit that they had tears in their eyes.

"Mr. Williams, why are they crying?" whispered one student. "We aren't that bad."

After singing five or six songs, the kids passed out the

yarn dolls. Some people cried over the gift, some hugged them, and a few tried to eat them. I could only assume the residents felt forgotten and were grateful for any attention at all.

We went back a month or two later and I passed out some of the pictures I had taken.

"That's me, but I wasn't there that day."

The poor man had no memory of our earlier visit.

On another of our visits a resident took a student to his room and locked the door. The man must have mistaken the boy for a puppy because he wanted to keep him.

Back at school I read an e-mail from the guidance counselor asking if she could speak to my class. It was Career Week, so she wanted to talk to the sixth graders and show them brochures on a variety of careers. I still had to be there for crowd control but had no teaching duties that day.

After talking about different job choices and the importance of job preparation, vocational school, apprenticeship, or college, she placed several brochures on a table and asked the students to read about various jobs, their duties, and average salaries.

Chris Conley said he wanted a brochure about being a waiter because he thought it would be a good way to meet men. He also asked one girl to trade seats with him so he could play footsie with the boy next to her.

The next morning, as usual, I stood by my classroom door as the students entered.

I noticed Justin Vinall walking toward my room. He waved at me and turned away to go to his own homeroom. He did that yesterday too, both before and after school. I could easily be overestimating my popularity, and believed most of my students liked me, but I could not recall students from other homerooms ever doing that before.

The next three or four mornings he walked into my classroom about ten minutes before the morning bell just to chat about nothing in particular. I had to turn him away the following morning because I was having a parent conference.

That day Justin handed me a note.

Dear Mr. Williams,

I like your class a lot and wish you were my father. My

real father died three years ago. I live with my mother and three

sisters. You seem nice and I like learning about other countries.

Justin

How could I turn away a student who wrote that? It's why I became a teacher in the first place.

The biggest laugh of my career came when I was telling my homeroom we might not be able to go on a field trip to a local museum because we did not have enough chaperones after two parents cancelled a few days before the trip.

One of my brighter students suddenly started singing,

"Potato, potatoe, tomato, tomatoe!

Let's call the whole thing off."

I howled and had to sit on top of someone's desk because I was laughing too hard to stand.

We did go on the field trip because another teacher had more chaperones than needed and gave us two.

We have three Teacher Workdays/Student Holidays each year that are scheduled to fall a few days before Report Card Day. Even though report cards are generated by computers, we still had to enter the grades, give behavior grades, and write comments. Some of those Workdays are taken up with meetings or instructional presentations.

Mrs. Harris called us into the library for an instructional session on accountability and teacher evaluations.

"I want to begin by asking you not to kill the messenger. I know you're not going to be happy with this but it's coming from high above. For the record, I don't like it either. Every principal in the county was given one of these iPads. It has sixty, that's right sixty items we're supposed to look for when we go into your classrooms.

Starting next year, principals are supposed to make five random informal observations and two scheduled formal ones. I've got booklets for all of you to explain what each of those items mean. We mark 'yes' and 'no' for the items that we see.

For example, look at the first item, Lesson Topic. If you begin a lesson by saying, 'Today we're going to learn about fractions,' I have to mark 'no' for lesson topic. It has to be written and displayed for everyone to read, AND it has to include the criteria for mastering the lesson. For example, you could say the students will be able to recognize a denominator, or the students will be able to solve four out of five problems when adding fractions. Even that will earn you no credit unless I see you point to the lesson topic sometime during the lesson.

I know," she said looking at the incredulous expressions on our faces.

"Look down at item 12, Student Praise. If you say, 'Elizabeth, you are the most brilliant student in the room, you had a perfect score on your last test, I'm super impressed with you,' I have to give you a 'no' for praise. In order to get a 'yes,' I have to hear you say, 'You met the goal for today's lesson.'

At the end of each observation the results will be automatically e-mailed to you, so you'll know instantly how you did. The informal observations won't count but your formal ones will.

Your observation scores and your students' scores on the state test will give you an overall score. Low scores will be considered grounds for dismissal. This is serious folks.

Remember, this starts next year. Now that I've ruined your day, you can go back to the peace and quiet of your empty classroom, or find another teacher to vent with."

Very little work was done that day as a pall hovered over the school.

Teaching social studies as a reading class means more book work but once in a while I still managed to fit in a mini-lecture. We covered Ancient Greece, complete with Greek Day and moved on to the Ancient Romans.

"Today I'm going to tell you about Ancient Roman entertainments.

I deliberately did not display today's lesson topic, nor did I point to where it should be. I held out as long as I could.

"Roman baths were usually the largest and fanciest buildings in most towns. They were more than just places to bathe. Besides hot, medium, and cool pools, they also had weight-lifting rooms, massage rooms, barbershops, game rooms, lecture rooms – no, Alice, that's not where I would hang out – snack bars, art galleries, gardens, and even libraries. Women had their own sections that were usually smaller than the men's. Many people went…"

"Eric McCoy, please report to the clinic. It's time for

your medicine," said the voice over the intercom.

"I'm tired of all those announcements! As I was saying, many people went to the baths every day. It was considered a social activity so people usually went there with a friend. Another popular pastime was going to the arena to watch a gladiator fight. Some of the matches might be gladiators against gladiators, gladiators against animals, or even animals against animals. Most gladiators were enemy soldiers captured during a war and turned into slaves. They were scary looking too – even scarier than Tyson."

Tyson laughed loudest of all because he knew it was a joke.

"Gladiators were offered their freedom and a reward if they fought hard enough. They might be killed if they fought poorly. The crowd might love it, but their managers did not. Gladiators were hard to replace."

"Steve Edwards, your mother brought your library book to the office. Please come get it."

"Shut up! Ahhhh! I want to rip that thing out of the wall! I give up! How do they expect me to teach like this?

Read pages 73 to 81 in your textbook."

"You go girl!" said Chris Conley.

It took a few minutes before I could stop laughing. That was certainly a mood changer.

Marco Rossi was as close to a swarthy hunk as you could ever find in the sixth grade. Most boys did not button the top button of their shirts, Marco didn't button the top three. Girls were crazy about this junior Italian stallion. The olive-skinned youth was often dragged into the bushes for kissing sessions. He pretended to protest but his words did not have much conviction. He lived with his divorced father who ran a nightclub and looked like a stud.

Gloom settled over the sixth grade girls when Marco announced he would be moving in three days to live with his mother.

During lunch period the principal asked Mrs. Hazen and I to gather our girls together and step out into the hallway.

Mrs. Harris led us to the girls' restroom where Juan, the head custodian, was waiting. She opened the door and called, "Is anyone in here?"

When no one answered, she led us inside. I felt very self-conscious being in what was normally off-limits territory.

"As you can see," said Mrs. Harris, "someone is leaving behind lipstick stains. I know most of you don't wear lipstick but those of you who do need to stop kissing the mirrors. It's making extra work for the janitors."

To demonstrate, Juan dipped his squeegee into a toilet and swiped it across the mirror.

It was hard not to chuckle at the looks of horror on the faces of some of the girls.

For the record, girls' restrooms look cleaner and do not smell as bad as the boys' restrooms. Boys are notorious for having bad aim.

Hat Day rolled around. After paying my dollar and receiving the rubber stamp on the back of my hand, I wore my oversized black magician's hat with the white stuffed rabbit on the brim.

I walked down the hallway and a third grader said,

"You wear that hat all the time!"

All the time! I suddenly understood how women with an overflowing closet could say, 'but I don't have a thing to wear.' This was only the third time I ever wore that hat. All the time, really?

I enjoyed the teaching part of being a teacher, but did not like all the bureaucratic red tape, regulations, and micromanaging that came with it. Most parents were reasonable and wanted what was best for their child. Fewer than one in ten seemed to relish conflict and make unreasonable demands insisting that the school cater to their petty whims. All of that, plus the new evaluation procedures, made teachers crave summer break even more than the students did. In fact, some students did not like summer breaks because it means not seeing many of their friends for two months and, even worse, being enrolled in day-care.

Judy Swaggart was slightly plump, physically mature, and functioned academically at a third grade level. She had been given social promotions because she obviously would not fit into a third grade class. On the last day of school she wore a low-cut dress showing cleavage and asked to see the D.A.R.E. officer.

Drug Abuse Resistance Education was a program, taught by a real police officer, to encourage students not to use illegal drugs.

I gave her permission, hoping someone in the office would notice she was not following the dress code. I had enough experience to know that if I complained someone could say, 'Why are you looking at a student's breasts?'

About an hour and a half later, the school secretary came around to tell us in private that one of the custodians had been arrested for molesting Judy and we were not to talk about it, especially to the reporters gathering in front of the school.

I found out later that Judy had told the D.A.R.E. officer that she and a friend came back on campus yesterday to play on the playground. It was a hot day so they walked into the building to get a drink of water and noticed that my classroom door was open because the custodian was cleaning the room. They saw the yearbooks that I had put on each desk after school and sat down to look at it. Judy claimed the custodian walked up behind her and felt up her breast.

All evening the teaser on the TV news was, "School janitor arrested on the last day of school for molesting a student. The full story at eleven." The actual story contained no new information except it named the janitor, Juan Ribeiro, age 58.

TEN

EXPERIENCE IS THE BEST TEACHER

or

THINGS I HAVE LEARNED

or

RAMBLINGS

Experienced teachers know that the number one predictor

of how well a child does in school is his or her address.

Typically students from upper-middle class families are more

likely to be successful at school than students from other

neighborhoods. That is partly because those families travel more and give their children a wider variety of experiences, but even more importantly, they place a higher value on education. Students from upper class families are often used to having things done for them and do not want to put in the effort. Working class families say education is important, but too often fail to follow through choosing immediate gratification over anything to do with school.

Civilization is based on the principle of delayed gratification. We plant seeds in hopes of a bountiful harvest in the future. We spend years getting an education in hopes of a better life in the future. Stanford University explored this idea with the Marshmallow Test. Four to six-year-old children were offered a marshmallow or cookie they could eat immediately, or they could have two if they waited fifteen minutes. Not only did those who held out get the extra treat, but follow-up studies showed they were more successful in life.

Reading is essential in the world we live in, but you already know that if you are reading this. Becoming a good reader often begins long before a child gets to school. Lying in a cozy bed or being comfortably held in someone's arms while being read to encourages the love of reading. Often, children love hearing the same story over and over again. I have heard that some aristocratic European families put a dab of honey on a book's cover for their infants to lick so they would fall in love with the physical book. If you tell a child about the importance of reading but they never see you reading, it is hard for them to believe that you really mean it. Setting an example of reading in front of your children is much more effective. Let the child read to you. Read to each other. Reading for pleasure is a good sign of intelligence.

Parent-Teacher conferences are seldom fun. Most teachers care and want what is best for students, but there are always a few bad members of any profession. From time to time, disagreements can arise, even among reasonable, good people. The first contact should be with the teacher, not the principal. Call ahead and make an appointment. It is always a bad approach to go into any parent-teacher conference in attack mode filled with rage, or with the intent of making demands. That only puts the teacher on the defensive and the teacher's goal then comes 'how can I get this person to shut up and get out of here,' instead of helping the student. The best approach is one of co-operation. How can **WE** (together) resolve this? If the conflict is still not resolved, then calmly go to the principal. Anger is not productive and leads to resentments.

It is hard to have a good life without a happy home. A home is much more than just a place to sleep and eat. A true home is a sanctuary where people feel both wanted and safe. Home is a place where people spend quality time with each other.

Critical thinking, problem solving, and independent thought are educational buzz words that schools like to throw around to impress both parents and the public at large, but I have seen very little evidence that they are really valued. School administrators dislike controversy, and teachers and professors who say they love it when their students disagree with them only mean it if the student comes around to their way of thinking by the end of the class period. Freedom of thought scares people.

There are ways you can encourage children to think for themselves. Start slow. You might not want to ask a four-year-old to go into a closet and pick out whatever they want to wear that day. Begin by holding up two outfits and asking which one they like best. Move on by asking the child to tell one good thing and one bad thing that happened that day. Listen. Hearing the bad things will give you a clue of what their problems are. Instead of asking do you like this book, movie, picture, event, scene, etc., ask *what* do you like or dislike, and *why* do you like or dislike it? Listen, listen, listen rather than correct or argue. Discuss, but do not argue when they answer a question you asked. Arguing will understandably make them reluctant to answer your questions.

It's not good to plan every moment of your child's life and constantly see that they are entertained or occupied. Boredom is a good teacher. It encourages them turn inward to seek solutions.

It's your job to discover who the child is, not to mold him or her into your ideal image. If you must shape them, limit it to encouraging kindness, consideration of others, and safety. Knowledge and intelligence are very important, but most important of all is being a good person. Ask your children what they have done to put a smile on someone's face today.

Responsibility comes much more from experience than from age. It is probably a good idea to remind a five-year-old not to forget his or her sweater when he or she goes outside to play in cold weather. By the time a child is twelve they should be responsible enough to remember it on their own. If not, let them experience real world consequences of their actions. Yes, they will be uncomfortable but after a few times, he or she will remember. You are not doing the child a favor by repeatedly reminding them of simple things. Instead of helping, you are enabling him or her to stay helpless and become an irresponsible adult who forgets his or her sweater. If you remind them nearly every time, there is no need for them to ever assume responsibility for themselves. Responsibility comes much more from experience than from age.

Freedom and responsibility go hand in hand. Freedom means doing whatever you want with the responsibility of not interfering with someone else's freedom. How loud can you play your music? Just short of bothering the people around you. Consideration for others is the whole basis of morality. Moral education should begin at home.

It sometimes takes a firm backbone to teach responsibility. I heard one behavior specialist offer this advice on discipline to parents. He said to inform the child that anything left on the floor is trash. Give them time to clean, and anything still left on the floor gets donated to charity or thrown out. Nagging annoys everyone and is unnecessary. You must follow through or what you say will not be believed. Cluttering shared areas interferes with other people's enjoyment of the home. Everyone should participate in doing their fair share of the chores. Tell the child to empty the trash, or fill the dishwasher, or do the laundry before dinner and do not mention it again. Do not set a plate for them until it is done. Or tell them to do something before going to bed and if it is not done, do not let them sleep. Of course, this only works if they want to go to bed. This can be done by making noise or even putting ice cubes in their bed. The technique should only be reserved for their fair share of chores and never used as a power display to show who is in control. The child might be angry and it might take a few times to learn you mean business, but they will eventually learn responsibility. Children should never rule the home.

Teach your children to respect experience and age. That begins by not calling adults by their first names until that person invites you to do so. Older people have wisdom to share if young people are smart enough to listen. Respect means to treat people like they are important. Children should not be allowed to disrespect their parents or elders. Rebellion is a normal part of adolescence, but it is possible to disagree without being disagreeable. You have the power of the purse, do not fail to use it. Also teach your children to respect all workers. We live in an interdependent world. I do not know anyone who built the home they live in, makes their own clothes, car, furniture, and grows their own food. We NEED other people. It is OK to think I am glad I do not have to do that, but it is not OK to look down on anyone doing an honest job. It is reasonable to object to people who lie, cheat, steal, bully, etc. but it is never reasonable to object to people because of who they are (occupation, race, sexuality, etc.).

Self-esteem is important for everyone because if we think of ourselves as failures, why should we try to do anything? Real self-esteem comes from achievement and success. Praising everything someone does gives a false self-esteem that leads to arrogance and entitlement. Who wants to be around people like that? It might be a good thing to construct situations where the child can be successful, but fake praise is never a good thing. Praise is an important motivator, and a great reward, and should be used often, but ONLY for real success. Nothing good comes from phony praise. Participation trophies are worthless. Constructive criticism also has value, but praise more often than criticize. Not only is it good to give a child praise when they deserve it, but it is also important to teach a child to give praise.

Saying 'please,' 'thank you,' 'excuse me,' and 'I'm sorry,' are great ways to show consideration for other. Giving compliments and general good manners, are things all people should practice and should be taught to children. It makes people a lot more pleasant to be around. The number one predictor of happiness is good relationships. I heard of one study that showed giving compliments improves your mood. I also heard of another study that said couples who say 'thank you' to each other were much more likely to be happy in their marriage and much less likely to divorce. Who doesn't like being appreciated? The whole idea of being 'completely natural' or 'letting it all hang out' is not a good one. Many disgusting things come out of the human body (and mind) and should remain private. I would much rather smell someone's cologne than their body odor. I would much rather hear silence than 'that is the ugliest shirt I've ever seen,' even if it is true.

All people should know where their food comes from. When asked where food comes from, too many young students answer the grocery store, and they are not trying to be funny. Children need the experience of seeing seeds planted, watching them grow, and harvesting something edible. Finicky eaters are much more willing to try a food if they have seen it growing. If a family does not have a flower bed to grow vegetables, they can be grown in a pot on a balcony, or even a pot in front of a window. Radishes, carrots, tomatoes, and cucumbers are all easy to grow. Not only are fresh vegetables healthier but it teaches the importance of taking care of the planet.

Students need to learn that life is not fair. Not everyone will win a first-place trophy. Winners are not people who never fall down, winners are people who get back up. Failure can be a powerful teacher. It is good for children to experience failure. Brave does not mean not being afraid, it means not letting fear stop you. Some people are born healthier, some are born stronger, some are born better looking. Many people who suffer a tragedy ask, 'why me?' but a more reasonable question is 'why not you?' Life is a series of random meaningless events. Bad things happen to good people. Life is not fair. Some of the most powerful lessons in life come out of pain. You learn to truly value people after you have lost someone. Sickness teaches the value of good health and teaches you not to take it for granted. Children (adults too) need to learn that just because we want something does not mean it is good for us. I want cream-filled or jelly-filled donuts every day. Life is full of struggles and that is hard on one's spirit. There is also beauty in the world whether it is a mountain, a tree, a brook, a flower, or a sunset. If it is not apparent, search for it and let your soul feast on it.

The only thing in life that can be guaranteed with absolute certainty is that things will change. No matter how bad or good your life is, it will change, whether you want it to or not. Bad times do not last forever, neither do good times.

People often feel isolated even though technology connects us. To build family unity, I heard about one celebrity who forced her squabbling children to sit next to each other on a couch and not let them get up until they could believably say 'I love you' to their sibling. It worked, as adults they were all close to each other. We have all seen people sitting in groups and not speaking to each other because they are texting on their phones. Connected to other people, yet not truly connected. Cellphones should *never* be out at the dinner table unless you are eating alone. They should also never make an appearance during a face-to-face visit with someone. If it is an emergency, excuse yourself and walk away. Making eye contact with someone should take priority over electronic social media. Friends and family are perhaps the most important things in your life but chose well. It is better to be lonely than with the wrong friends.

Helicopter parents is a term for parents who hover over their kids, watching and controlling everything they do. Bulldozer parents are even worse because they try to remove all obstacles in their child's way. Both types have good intentions but are harming their children more than helping them by robbing them of developing independence. Good parenting means providing food, clothing, and shelter, making your child feel wanted, educating him or her, making them likeable (good manners), and making them independent and able to function on their own. It is a huge mistake to think the school will handle everything about educating your child.

ELEVEN

All summer long the main topic on the teachers'

grapevine was Juan Ribeiro and what was happening to him. In

no way could we condone what he was accused of, but we also

could not imagine him ever doing it. Juan was a very religious

man, plus he had a heart attack eight months before the

accusation.

He was held in jail for four days before he was bailed out.

Juan's wife could not speak English and had trouble

understanding what was going on but stood with him.

Of course he lost his job, so he was left with no income.

After he came home, people would drive past his small house

with their horns blasting making it hard to sleep. His neighbors would yell at him when he set foot out of his house. Very little had changed by the time school resumed again.

Richard Freeman, the itinerant band teacher who used to work at Kenwood, and I became friends. He, his wife, and I went out to dinner about three weeks into the new school year.

"Why didn't I see you at the PTA's Welcome Back get-together?" I asked.

"Ann's brother's family came over that night. Did I miss anything?"

"Not really, but the PTA board has a different *feel* to it this year. In the past the PTA was about 'what can we do to help the school,' this year it's more 'I've done this project and volunteered for that committee, so I want this favor or that favor, and I want my kid put in that teacher's class.' I hope that's not a national trend."

"Ohhh, this beef stroganoff is delicious!" said Ann. "Did Richard tell you about our trip to Madeira?"

"I don't believe so."

"My brother married a Portuguese girl who told us about

it. It's a tiny island in the Atlantic Ocean about six hundred miles from Lisbon. It's very mountainous and extremely beautiful. It's where this Madeira comes from," she said, holding up a wine glass.

"The food is great there, the climate is ideal, and we signed up for a few scenic tours. Our guide was also named Richard, Richard Matos. I can't wait to go back again. The only bad thing is you have to take an eight-hour flight to Lisbon, and then a nearly two-hour flight to the island."

"It's a good thing you're both teachers, so you have summers off. I got my master's degree this summer, so I'll have time to travel next summer. Some of my happiest moments have been in the audience of a theater. I want to see a few Broadway shows in Manhattan."

"Congratulations, are you planning to become a principal?"

"That was the plan when I started but I hate confrontation and that's half of what being a principal means. I'm just proud to be the first member of my family to get a master's degree."

"Have you thought about what you want to order for

dessert?" asked Ann.

"I love their Boston Cream Pie, but I'm afraid I'm going to pass. At *best* my figure can be described as 'relaxed-fit.' The other day at school a kindergarten kid patted my stomach and asked when my baby was due."

"Oh, you're not overweight," said Ann.

"This one is a keeper, hang on to her," I said to Richard. "I know I have a pouch but resent it being called a beer belly. I don't even like beer. Now, in an effort to change the subject, do you remember me telling you about the time Marie McGuinness and I went to a fortune teller?"

"Yes, then you went to another one who told you the same thing."

"That's right. The first fortune teller's son is in my homeroom this year, and the other fortune teller is his grandmother. That's why their stories were the same. Mom taught the daughter. I asked him if he thought his mother could predict the future. He shook his head and gave me a look like he thought it was the dumbest question he had ever heard. How's everything at your school, Ann?"

"The same as every other school in Florida. We're trying to adapt to the new accountability system. We live in constant fear the principal might pop into our rooms for one of his ambush observations. No one likes to be judged. And when he does come, we have to go into a song and dance number, pointing here, saying that, trying to remember to phrase something in just the right way, all the time looking to see if the principal is watching or whether he has his head bent down looking at the iPad. It's horrible!"

"Exactly! It's like that at our school too," I agreed. "We have a good principal, but I fear seeing her walk down the hall."

"Last year the county banned baked goods from home because of peanut allergies, and this year parents can't even bring cupcakes and donuts from a bakery because only healthy treats are allowed."

"I know, but birthdays are special. I used to hand out hard candies as reward and that had to stop. I don't know about you, but one of my pet peeves is the constant interruption of intercom announcements. I think our secretary wants be a radio announcer."

"Don't forget the fire drills and lice outbreaks," added Ann.

"I think we're turning into a cliché," said Richard. "They say whenever teachers get together, they always talk about school."

"How do you guys deal with the lack of privacy? I run into students at the grocery store, the mall, the movies, everywhere I go in town. I like photography and one day I was flipping through a photography book in a bookstore and randomly came across a picture of a nude and heard, 'Mr. Williams!' I could feel my face turn bright red. When I got to school the next day, the kids already knew where I went, what I did, and even who I was with. I'm sure they'll know about tonight's dinner even though I don't see anyone else in here that I recognize."

"I remember being bothered by that in my earlier days," said Ann, "but you just get used to it after a while."

"I'm not there yet."

"Well, I've had a good time and enjoyed our conversation," said Richard. "We'll have to do this again some time."

This was my sixth year of teaching. While I don't claim to be an expert, I have learned the value of experience. I know what to expect and how to handle most situations. I will pick an experienced lawyer, doctor, dentist, or accountant over a beginner every time.

When winter break arrived, I stopped at a Chinese restaurant to get a take-out order of steamed dumplings and chicken and broccoli. I had just unloaded my car and collapsed into my recliner when the phone rang.

I instantly recognized the voice as Lori Sirota, a teacher from Kenwood.

"Oh my goodness, how are you?" I exclaimed.

"Today was our winter break party and it reminded me of you. Most of us just turn it over to our room mothers, but you always took a few kids to the grocery store and let them pick out their own goodies."

"Yes, but I'm not allowed to do that any longer. The way I understand it, and I might have it wrong, school insurance won't cover transportation in private vehicles. It's only OK if we go on a school bus. So how is everything at Kenwood these days?"

"Oh you know, food fights, spit balls, and lice, the same as always. I had something embarrassing happen the other day, you'll like this. We were studying about plants in science, so I took my class to the Banyan Florist and Nursery the other day. You know where that is. It's only about four blocks from the school. We were walking on one side of the street and on the other side of the street was a man in a dress, a wig, and full make-up strutting in our direction. Biceps that big do not belong in a dress. I couldn't help myself and laughed out loud. Actually it wasn't a laugh as much as it was a suppressed giggle. The more I tried to stop, the worse it got. I was embarrassed to act like that in front of my students. When we got back to our classroom, I apologized for losing control of myself. Some of my kids live in that area and didn't understand why I was giggling. They saw him all the time and thought it was a normal part of their neighborhood."

"I've got an embarrassing story for you. Your husband is Greek, so you might appreciate this. I'm teaching Western

Civilization in social studies and spend a lot of time on Greece. One of my students raised his hand in class and asked, 'My friend Barry is Greek, and he says he's *uncircumcised*, what does that mean?' To say I was shocked would be an understatement. All I could do was stammer out something about asking your parents at home. Looking back, I have no doubt that the little twerp just wanted to reduce me to a blubbering mass, and he did. At the time I wanted to strangle him but he's really a good kid who just wanted a harmless laugh. He was in my class last year and on the last day of school I caught him writing, 'Your son is very bright and a pleasure to have in class' on the back his report card. I started to scold him but realized that it was true."

"Whatever happened to that janitor from your school who got arrested? It was in the news all the time, but we haven't heard anything lately."

"Most of us don't think he did it and the teachers even took up a collection to help pay his lawyer. He's had a hard time of it. On his first night in jail, one of the cops told him, 'If I wasn't a policeman, I'd take you into the parking lot and beat the crap out of you.' There have been several court dates. Juan shows up but the girl doesn't. That means legal procedures have to be rescheduled and that just prolongs things even further. The judge even said that when the defendant misses so many court dates, the case would normally be dismissed but child molestation charges are too serious."

We talked over an hour about people we both knew and our shared dislike of the new accountability system and how it was a morale killer.

"You know, I heard of one high school teacher who staples Burger King job applications to failed test papers," she said.

"Really?"

"Probably not, but it's funny. Anyway, stay in touch. I've got to start dinner. I'm not sure what to cook tonight. Maybe I'll talk Mitch into taking me out."

I love to go to dinner, concerts, museums, and plays, but I am mostly a homebody. Give me a good book or a good TV show and I am perfectly happy to stay in. In fact, to me a fun evening would be a nice dinner, good conversation, and a great movie at home.

Tonight I was entertaining the Freemans again.

Like many only children I am more comfortable with people older or younger than with people my own age. I hang around with sixth graders all day so being friends with the Freemans who were about ten to fifteen years older did not feel unusual.

"I know we were just here two months ago, but something seems different," said Ann. "What's changed?"

"The Flying Mercury figurine over there is new. I got it when some friends and I went to Tarpon Springs a few weeks ago."

"I heard the good news about Juan Ribeiro," said Richard.

"What news?" asked Ann.

"Just yesterday, nearly fifty weeks after she make the accusation, Judy Swaggart admitted that she made the whole thing up," I answered. "She had a crush on the D.A.R.E. officer and she was afraid she wouldn't see him again. I knew something was fishy all along. You don't wear a low-cut dress if you've just been molested. Also, her friend was in the room at the time and did not see Juan touch her or ever hear her tell him to leave her alone."

"Can you imagine the nightmare that man's family has lived through?"

"They nearly lost their home, but their church stepped in and made their mortgage payments for them," I answered. "Juan's problems aren't over yet. The school board has agreed to give him his job back, at another school, but they don't want to give him backpay even though they fired him without just cause. His lawyer is going to challenge that. Do you know what scares me the most about this whole thing? It could just as easily have been me that she accused. Let me drop the pasta into the pot and I'll be right back."

"I'm sure Bret's on the phone with his girlfriend right now," said Ann.

"I hope Kyle's not giving him a hard time about it," said Richard. "We were just talking about our kids while you were in the kitchen. Something smells good."

"I'm making spaghetti and meatballs and hope you both like it. I put a little twist on it, I don't like onions and use a lot of garlic."

I put the food on the table and we gathered around.

"I once heard a Chinese chef say if you want a flavor to stand out you should only put it in one dish because it's the contrast that makes it stand out. I didn't do that today. There's garlic in the spaghetti sauce, garlic in the salad, and we have garlic bread. I'm crazy about garlic!"

"Speaking of crazy, that reminds me of something that recently happened at school," said Ann. "We're supposed to have one fire drill a month and they always happen at the worst time. At our last drill I said, 'These fire drills are driving me crazy. One of these days the men in the white coats are coming to take me away to the funny farm.' The next day one of my students brought a large shopping bag into my class and insisted I stay away from it. After lunch he took it into the restroom and came out wearing a long white coat and said he had come to take me away. I couldn't help but laugh."

"I'll bet he was gifted. That's the kind of things they do. For a week or two one of my gifted students was calling me at 4:30 in the morning pretending to be anyone from an all-night dry-cleaner to a movie director who wanted me to star in one of her movies. She couldn't understand why I didn't appreciate her phone calls as much as she did. Her father was a baker and when he got up, the whole family got up. She was lonesome and I didn't want to hurt her feelings, so I asked the guidance counselor to speak to her. Three times I've had girls with crushes on me that I felt were too serious for me handle myself, so I asked the guidance counselor to deal with it. I don't know what she says to them but all three girls gave me the cold shoulder for the rest of the year."

"I don't have those problems," said Richard. "I only see the band kids two or three times a week. By the way, did you hear about Danny Thom dying in a car crash? I think he was at Kenwood when you were still there."

"Yes, I saw it in the newspaper. He wasn't in any of my classes but I vaguely remember him. I noticed that his obituary contained the phrase 'and he was an athlete' as if that made his loss even greater. I've never understood that. How is the loss of an athlete any worse than the loss of a band member, or a member of the drama club, or even a member of the chess club, and it is not as bad as the loss of a member of the honor society or debating club. I'm sure Danny was a good kid, but his death is not any more tragic because he was an athlete."

"His father is stationed overseas in the Navy so they are delaying the funeral until he can get here," added Richard. "And, can we talk about something other than kids dying?"

"You mentioned the military, that reminds me of a story," said Ann. "Back before the FCAT, we used to give handwriting grades. One man could not understand why his stepdaughter got an A for handwriting but a C on the actual assignment. He had recently married the girl's mother, so he wanted to make a display of being a concerned father. One morning before school, he came charging into my classroom like the ex-marine that he was."

"How did you handle that?" I asked.

"I was only a little scared to *death*. I'm glad we have marines fighting for us, but don't like them fighting against us. The man never did understand the difference between the two grades, but he put on a display in front his stepdaughter and that's all he really wanted. I never heard from him again."

"He clearly overreacted but the role of men and women has changed over the years and sometimes men don't know how to act," suggested Richard. "Calling a thirty-year-old man a boy was always considered an insult but calling a thirty-year-old woman a girl was considered a compliment because women were more sensitive about their age. That's no longer true. Some of us were taught that we were supposed to be the breadwinners and head of the household. With the equality of women, we don't know what our role is. We were taught to open doors for women. Some women like it but some get angry, 'are you suggesting I'm too weak to open my own door, I'm perfectly capable of taking care of myself.'"

"That's happened to you?" asked Ann.

"No, but I saw it happen to someone else."

"It's just good manners. I hope you don't stop opening the door for me. Oh, did I tell you I have my first ever transgender student this year?"

"Another school story," moaned Richard.

"I'll ignore that."

"I thought you might."

"What's the difference between transgender and transsexual?" I asked.

"I'm not sure, I don't even know if there is one. This kid was born a boy but around age two or three told his parents that he was really a girl. From the beginning he liked dolls more than trucks. Luckily for him, his parents are very supportive. They let him dress any way he wants at home, but he has to dress like a boy when he steps outside because they don't want him to be bullied. He still lives as a boy but plans to transition between elementary and middle school."

"Has he been put on puberty blockers yet?"

"Oh yes."

"How do you deal with him in the classroom?"

"The same way I deal with any other kids. I try to give him acceptance and protect him from bullies. The only real difference is that he uses the teachers' restroom instead of the boys' room."

"I had identical twin brothers one year. One was gay, the other one wasn't. The other kids could tell them apart but most teachers couldn't. They came to school one day wearing identical shoes and pants but different colored shirts. The plan was to go to their own classes in the morning, switch shirts in the bathroom, and go to their brother's classes in the afternoon," I explained. "They almost got away with it, but I noticed a slight difference in their eyes. I stood in front of the class and said, 'Before I begin today's lesson I want to ask if anyone knows the two most important cities in Ancient Greece? What about you Edgar, since you heard me talk about them in second period?' Edgar's eyes widened, he knew he had been caught."

"I'm an only child and was always jealous of identical twins," said Ann. "I always asked them if they were each other's best friends. They always said 'no,' but whenever you saw them on the playground or anywhere else, they were always together."

"I'm an only child too. I've always thought it would be great to have someone who saw life the same way you do. The twins were both nice kids, but puberty wasn't very kind to them. They both developed bad cases of B.O. They were not in my homeroom but because I was the only male teacher in sixth grade, I was given the task of talking to them about it. No one ever warned me that was part of the job."

"I just remembered something," said Richard. "I had a band student who named his cat Dee-R-E-A, but he spelled it diarrhea."

"Really?"

"No, but you guys were telling funny stories so I wanted to tell one too. I heard an ice skater on TV say that. Say, do you remember Carol Duplantis?"

"Yes, she was in my low math group. Not exactly a Rhodes Scholar, that one."

"More like a Road Scholar," commented Richard. "She was arrested along Citrus Boulevard for solicitation."

I was glad to see summer break finally arrive. It is wonderful to wake up in the morning and be free to do whatever I pleased. There were always a few students I missed, and I added a few more notes to my collection.

Mr. Williams,

I have enjoyed you as a teacher very much this year. I wish I had you last year because I hated her. She always picked on me when I didn't do anything. Hope to come visit you

next year.

Love,

Brad

To Mr. Williams,

  You have told me many things, about Greece, England, and other parts of Europe. I have never had a teacher like you. You're truly one-of-a-kind. I admire you as you are and I admire your style. If I ever became a teacher (which I hope I won't), I would want to be just like you. Nice when there's time and strict when there isn't. Funny when you want to be, and sometimes grouchy. Yes, you are a man of many moods and quite a personality. You are (as my opinion) of the higher class. You are not too dignified or stuck-up like the other teachers. When we ask you to state your opinion or to have a serious talk, it's serious. If you should quit teaching many children will be disappointed. You are a one-of-a-kind guy.

"Unique" is the word, and I want other people to meet you. I
hope I'll see you next year!

Your Admirer,

Ted

I've seen many changes in my career. Some good, most were not. There were forty students in my first class. Now class sizes have been reduced to about half that. The worst change was the state over-regulating schools. Teacher enthusiasm is one of our greatest tools and being micromanaged from bureaucrats and administrators kills that.

The micromanaging, morale killing accountability system was introduced to us by telling us to think of education as a three-legged stool. The three legs are: curriculum (what we teach), methodology (how we teach), and relationship. Relationship means the more a student likes the teacher, the more likely he/she is to learn from that teacher. That is why mentorship is an effective method of teaching. The accountability system concentrates on the first two legs and ignores the third leg even though research shows that relationship is the most powerful. The statewide test regards students as being little more than data. They have been reduced to test scores and whether they go up or down and by how much. It has been in place for several years and if it is so great, why are the SAT scores not going up? Science is very reliable in many areas, but teaching is more of an art than a science. Science might be able to determine that one teaching method works better than another under specific conditions, but how can it create curiosity, motivation, relationship, or the ability to manage people without them resenting it. It is not possible for one test to encompass everything. Penmanship has gone down in priority because it was not on the statewide test. At the time of this writing, neither was civics. No one in this country should be able to graduate high school without knowing the three branches of government, what a constitution is, or how the President and Congressional Representatives are selected.

After a while we develop resistance, but beginning teachers catch every contagious illness going around. Teachers these days have to deal with school shootings, illegal drugs, helicopter parents, and students who feel entitled because they have been overly praised and given trophies just for showing up.

Even students have changed. Perhaps it was just the neighborhood where I taught but students had a negative attitude toward school, a punishment for being young, and considered both parents and - especially - teachers as the enemy. Over the years students became much less rebellious, more passive, more dependent, and helpless, at least at the elementary level. When I started teaching most boys seemed to have no interest at all in clothes, blue jeans and t-shirts were the standard uniform. Years later I saw a group of boys bring another boy to tears all because he was wearing the wrong brand of shirt and shoes.

There is a popular saying among teachers that half of all beginning teachers permanently leave the profession within the first five years. I don't know if that is really true, but too many do quit because of low pay and feeling unappreciated. We can get ten compliments and one complaint, but it is the complaint that we take home with us. I've also heard that teachers have a high rate of divorce and alcoholism. Ask any experienced teacher and they will be able to tell you stories similar to these.

After thirty-nine years as a teacher, I retired. Over the years I have had hundreds of students and have accidentally been called 'mom' and received more proposals than I can count. I heard about of some of my former students going to jail and some dying. One became Teacher of the Year in the ninth largest school district in the United States (I taught her husband too). At least one is a professional opera singer, at least one became an airline pilot, and at least one is listed in IMBD (International Movie Data Base). I have no idea how many became physicians, politicians, scientists, community leaders, or teachers. I just hope they are kind, decent, happy citizens.

My three favorite moments in teaching are those 'aha' moments when you see a student's face light up because he or she suddenly *gets* the lesson; those all too rare moments when I am lecturing or telling a story and every eye and ear is on me eagerly waiting for what I am going to say next; and, best of all, when former students come back to visit. That is when you know you made a difference.

TWELVE

Letters from parents and former students

(and assignments about past teachers)

Dear Mr. Williams,

I am pleased to inform you that I kept Jane out of school yesterday because of a cough due to a cold. Will you please accept this excuse?

Mr. Smith

Dear Mr. Williams,

My son Jeff had to stay home because of a good reason.

Thank you,

Mrs. Smith

Please excuse Jane from school yesterday. She had a tooth removal.

Thank you,

Mrs. Smith

Dear Mr. Williams,

My name is John Jones, Jane's stepfather and I would like to know how is it that Jane is failing in Spelling. She haven't at anytime come home with Spelling homework.

Mr. Jones

To Mr. Williams

This is inform you that Jane have work very hard trying to get this work but i don't think she under stand it and I tried to help her but I don't have the nerve left I know She tried I told her to ask For help to under stand it but I guess She didn't Sincerely

Mrs. Smith

Mr. Williams,

Jane told me that you put her name on the Board for not turning in a Report. We both know that that report was about Saturn. I spent Fri. & Sat. Nite learning What to Write about. I hope you read it. And I also hope you like it because her and I spent some time on it.

I hope the report didn't get misplaced and I also hope it didn't affect Jane's grade. We didn't mess around I swear we did it. And I hope this note get our point across and doesn't make me sound like A fool.

Thank you

Jane's Sister

Dear Mr. Williams,

Jeff and I want to tell you how much Jeffy enjoyed your class and admired you as a person as well as a teacher. It was so nice to have him excited about a class, as he was about yours. You have a very special way with students, and we appreciate all you did for Jeffy.

Thank you for everything and have a nice summer.

Sincerely,

Alice

Dear Mr. Williams,

I would like to extend to you my deepest appreciation for making Jeff's school year so exciting. Out of 5 children none of them has ever shown such excitement about learning.

I thank God for teachers who love their profession, it means so much to the children.

May God Bless you this coming year

Mrs. Smith

Dear Mr. Williams,

My wife and I wanted to thank you for helping make Jeff's year at Princsonia both enjoyable and scholastically valuable. We have been please with his scholastic progress and feel that his experiences in Princsonia have prepared him for the seventh grade.

Also, I hope you can appreciate the great pride and joy we both felt today when he received the "Faculty Award." I, personally, have never before experience such a sensation of pride. We thank you both for Jeff and us.

The fact that he received the award is reflective of the fine job done by his teachers.

I have written identical letters to all of Jeff's teachers. Please do not interpret this as apathy – I hope you understand it is hard to find appropriate words for all of you. Again, thank you.

Very truly yours,

Mr. Smith

Dear Mr. Williams,

Just a note to say thank you for what you've done for Jane. She has improved so much over the past year and I know that your teaching methods/skills/enthusiasm or whatever it is, is largely responsible.

I don't think I'd be a good parent, considering the times, if I had not read one of your letters to her. (Besides she left it open on the dining room table.) I was delighted that you wrote her back and that you encouraged her to read. I can't thank you enough.

Well basically, that's all I wanted to say, except that I hope you will continue to do as you have done. From where I stand you are an excellent mentor And I will always consider your contribution to Jane's upbringing, A+.

Mrs. Smith

P.S. You know of course that there's another daughter coming your way. ETA 5 years.

Dear Mr. Williams,

I would just like to tell you thank you for all that you have taught me. It has helped me so much throughout this past school year. I've been making nothing but A's in both language arts (mostly because of your "creative writing" assignments and Geography. I wouldn't have known half of the things I know if it wasn't for you. I enjoyed being in your class and I miss it very much. You made social studies fun. Bust most importantly, you taught me something that could never be found in a book ……you taught me that you could be friends with your teacher.

Sincerely, Your appreciative student, Travis Lemaster

Dear Brenford,

    Or should I say "Dear Kentucky Colonel"?! I want in my own way to tell you how happy I am that both Jeff and I had the privilege of having known and cared for you! – I was very serious when I said Jeff related to you – and I'm grateful you are you – and allowed him to express himself. I thank you for your perception and kindness to my very special child. His life won't always be easy – but at least this year was a good one for him – one he seems to especially remember with good feelings. You allowed enough "craziness," enough "emotion" of your own to show especially at a time he needed to know this was OK in a man! Thank you so much! Be Happy

Love

Mrs. Smith

Mr. Williams, you have been dancing around in my mind a lot lately. Not literally of course. There's an explanation for this: I've been reading a lot more than usual. I feel like reading is my stress reliever. It's my go-to for anything honestly. I've read Last Lecture, by Randy Pausch. I'm also reading Tuesdays with Morrie, by Mitch Albom. Both of which are very inspirational reads. So whilst reading these books, I've noticed that each of these people had a mentor, or someone they looked up to, particularly in Tuesdays with Morrie. And I would say to myself how amazing it would be to have someone like that in my life. And then I think of you and your impact on my life, and how I miss that. I truly want you to know that I'm grateful for you as a person as well as being there for me and being the someone I looked up to. That's why you've danced around so frequently in my mind. Other than that, nothing has been going on. I picked up basketball, I wasn't sure if you knew that or not. Is is one of the sports I actually do quite enjoy, that and crew. (Rowing, which they offer in Colorado!) I've picked up piano again and I'm learning The Nocturnes by Chopin. (there's quite a few if I do recall.) Tuesday is my last day, I'm sad and happy at the same time. Both dull words to describe my feelings leaving a dull place with beautiful, kind people. I really hope you finish your novel. I would love to read it. You have to tell me what it's about or give me a teaser or something. What's it called? How long have you been working on it? What genre is it? We never got to play our chess game by the way. I've played a lot of strategy games lately and of all that has stuck. Something about the complexity of it that intrigued me to keep playing. I won't boast, but I do hope we eventually get to sit down and chat over a friendly cut of coffee or tea and chess. I hope to see you soon my old friend. Take care.

Dear Mr. Williams,

        I'm writing this letter for two reasons one is because you're one of my favorite teachers and also it is an assignment. I remember how you were very strict about turning work in, but that has helped me a lot this year. I have all A's in every class, my world cultures teacher wants me to test for gifted, and tell Mrs. Tucker that I'm in advanced math. You could say

I'm having a pretty good year. I also had to do alot of reviews

over the summer and that helped me too. I really like it here in

middle school and what I told you at the top of the letter forget it.

You are my favorite teacher.

Mike Wilson

Mr. Williams

By Miles Webb

My favorite teacher would have to be Mr.

Williams, he was my sixth grade teacher. He was really nice,

calm, and had a since of humor. He always told jokes and used

different voices while he was reading to us. He teased people but

in a good way. Most if not all kids thought he was an awesome

teacher. Sixth grade is a year I will never forget, and I will also

never forget Mr. Williams.

I and a couple of friends try to go visit Mr. Williams

every once in a while. Last time we went he was in a teachers'

meeting. We're going to try again next week, probably on

Wednesday. I miss Mr. Williams and hope he's having a year as good as mine so far.

Made in the USA
Columbia, SC
21 June 2019